FIXIN' TO GET KILLED

The impact of the rifle slug punching a hole in the cabin's stovepipe brought Johnny Crowheart bolt upright. He made a grab for his holstered gun, only to drop the weapon when Ezra Morgan and his three sons shouldered into the cabin. Their hats shaded eyes lusting with the need to draw blood.

"We gonna hang him, Pa?" Jo Bob asked.

Johnny glanced at the big hunting knife hanging from Ezra Morgan's waist.

"Naw," Ezra said, his dark eyes gleaming with malice and hate. "More likely cut him to ribbons first!"

BEST OF THE WEST
from Zebra Books

THOMPSON'S MOUNTAIN   (2042, $3.95)
by G. Clifton Wisler

Jeff Thompson was a boy of fifteen when his pa refused to sell out his mountain to the Union Pacific and got gunned down in return, along with the boy's mother. Jeff fled to Colorado, but he knew he'd even the score with the railroad man who had his parents killed . . . and either death or glory was at the end of the vengeance trail he'd blaze!

BROTHER WOLF   (1728, $2.95)
by Dan Parkinson

Only two men could help Lattimer run down the sheriff's killers — a stranger named Stillwell and an Apache who was as deadly with a Colt as he was with a knife. One of them would see justice done — from the muzzle of a six-gun.

BLOOD ARROW   (1549, $2.50)

by Dan Parkinson
Randall Kerry returned to his camp to find his companion slaughtered and scalped. With a war cry as wild as the savages,' the young scout raced forward with his pistol held high to meet them in battle.

THUNDERLAND   (1991, $3.50)
by Dan Parkinson

Men were suddenly dying all around Jonathan, and he needed to know why — before he became the next bloody victim of the ancient sword that would shape the future of the Texas frontier.

Available wherever paperbacks are sold, or order direct from the Publisher. Send cover price plus 50¢ per copy for mailing and handling to Zebra Books, Dept. 2432, 475 Park Avenue South, New York, N.Y. 10016. Residents of New York, New Jersey and Pennsylvania must include sales tax. DO NOT SEND CASH.

ROBERT KAMMEN
WINTER OF THE BLUE SNOW

ZEBRA BOOKS
KENSINGTON PUBLISHING CORP.

ZEBRA BOOKS

are published by

Kensington Publishing Corp.
475 Park Avenue South
New York, NY 10016

First printing: August, 1988

Printed in the United States of America

For Marlene

Chapter One

In 1875 they migrated out of the Texas Panhandle, old Jake Murdock and one son and around twenty cowhands pushing along three thousand longhorns. The northward trek had taken its toll on both men and livestock. But shining strong in rancher Murdock was a vision of the Badlands, a strange and sheltered land he'd seen but once, and a self-made promise that after delivering the trail herd over to Miles City, he would strike eastward accompanied by his segundo, Bill Lowman.

On the afternoon of the second day, Bill Lowman reined his sorrel around a scrub oak, squinted slowly from under the stained brim of his brown Stetson at the rancher, and muttered, "Yesterday we crossed the Powder River. Meanin', Jake, we're just about runnin' out of Montana and there's still no sign of them . . . Badlands."

Folding his large, gnarled hands over the saddle horn as he pulled up, Jake Murdock surveyed the tawny plains stretching into the hazy distance. Murdock and his segundo were second-generation Texans, though at fifty he was a decade older than Bill Lowman. The seams in the rancher's flinty face had been eroded by harsh winters and heat-singed summers, by fist and rope and barbed wire. The probing eyes were rheumy blue, had been witness to more hard times than good, and Jake Murdock had hung his share of rustlers, be they whites or renegade Indians, along with some Mex banditos.

In a voice scoured by age and the elements he said, *"Les mauvaises terres a traverser*—bad lands to cross. The words of a Canuck trapper I bested at five card stud."

"According to General Sully the Badlands is hell with the fires burned out. I just can't cotton to a place like that, Jake."

"I felt the same way when first setting eyes upon the Badlands. But it's more than that, Bill, a whole heap more. The Sioux tell it differently." Loping eastward again, the rancher went on to narrate how once upon an ancient time the Badlands were a fertile plain, thick with buffalo grown fat on rich grasses. "It was a place of harmony where, each autumn, the tribes gathered to hunt and trade and hold friendly councils in the shade along the Little Missouri River. Though they were hostile elsewhere, here they met in peace.

"In Sioux legend," the rancher went on, "trouble came from the west. A fierce mountain tribe rode down to claim the hunters' paradise, driving the plains people out. They tried to reclaim it, but failed. Finally they met in a great council to fast and pray to the Great Spirit.

"After many days without an answer, they had begun to despair . . . when suddenly a great tremor seized the earth, the sky grew black as night, and lightning burned jagged through the gloom. Fires began to flame and sizzle underfoot, and the earth tossed and pitched like the waves of the sea. The mountains heights that were there sank smoking along with these invaders, as did the streams and trees and all that lived there. Then, just as abruptly as it had begun, the terror ended, leaving the plain in grotesque disarray. And thus it was that the Great Spirit destroyed the prize that had stirred up strife among his children, and the Badlands were born."

Bill Lowman was a shade over six feet, the years spent in the saddle having hammered the Texan into a hard sinewy slimness, and though possessed of a calm, easy manner, there'd been times when he'd bested men bigger'n him in fisticuffs. He had a dark, handsome complexion, and the black handlebar mustache curled upward at its flaring ends. The segundo was a bachelor but at age forty still had notions of getting hitched to a certain Texas woman. As segundo for Jake Murdock's Hashknife, Lowman simply figured it was his job to delegate authority, something he did without rancor and not favoring any particular cowhand working for him. Ranching was a daylong, and sometimes all-night, chore—the credo Bill Lowman lived by.

Oftentimes he'd been tempted to start his own spread. Lately, though, things had been tougher'n rawhide down in Texas, what with drought and low prices and this arduous task of having to bring up a trail herd to be sold at these northern markets nearly every summer. So he could understand why Jake Murdock wanted to relocate. But if it were him, Lowman knew, he'd be a-hankering to settle westward where them Big Horns shadowed the Wyoming plains.

The Stetson favored by Lowman had a long crease in its crown, with a tail feather from a red-tailed hawk in its faded reddish band, the front brim slanted down to shade chestnut-tinted eyes constantly scanning what lay fringing the limits of his vision. Both men wore leather vests, but Lowman's had a round paper tab dangling from a shirt pocket and being tossed about by the erratic wind tugging at his checkered shirt. It was a pleasant autumn day, perhaps in the low seventies, and partly cloudy.

Toward nightfall, and with long shadows dancing ahead to announce their presence, the rancher smiled at his first glimpse—bluish tinted buttes announcing a break in the endless prairie—of the place he sought. "A few ranches have already been established over there."

"Any from Texas?"

"Yup—the OX and 777 spreads."

"At least we'll have someone to palaver with."

"Still harboring doubts about this?"

"Not even longhorns could survive a winter out here on these plains. And that same snow'll sure as sin cover them Badlands."

"Bill"—Jake Murdock smiled—"it's my opinion somebody should have called them the Goodlands, 'cause it's an ideal place to raise cattle, winter or summer."

This statement only brought from Lowman a skeptical grimace as he trailed after the rancher, clucking his horse into a canter. A short distance later, Murdock drew rein on a rising stretch of prairie, and then Bill Lowman pulled up too and studied with some wonderment this strange barrier called the Badlands sunken below where he sat in the saddle. Instead of being such a place as the Grand Canyon, as he'd led himself to believe, there lay before the segundo verdant trees and lush grass twisting amongst heights being plated with gold by daylight's final glow. While the rancher was simply content to dismount and walk his horse closer to the edge of the rise, Bill Lowman, in that quick way of his, fished out his tobacco pouch and wad of paper, and then rolled a cigarette into shape before swinging his pondering eyes to Murdock.

"There's more to it than I reckoned. Different, too."

"Meaning I'm not that much of a fool for wanting to settle here?"

A grin played across the segundo's lips. "The jury's still out on that."

Chapter Two

Nearly a decade later, in 1886, the long winter was giving way to early spring. For the men of the Hashknife, tugged deep in the Badlands where Squaw Creek joined the Little Missouri River, this meant the chore of rounding up most of the horses let loose to shift for themselves during the winter, but chiefly that of hauling out mired cows and steers.

As long as everything was frozen solid there was little danger, except for a spring snowstorm, to the livestock. Spring thaw changed all of that: a time when the river ice broke up, the streams were left with an edging of deep bog, and when the quicksand was at its worst. As the frost melted out of the soil, the ground around the alkali springs changed into a trembling quagmire, and deep holes of slimy, tenacious mud formed in the bottom of all the gullies.

The cattle, which had been foraging through the thick-piled snow for grass, were gaunt and weakened, and craving water. They rushed heedlessly into any pool and stand while lapping greedily at the icy water as they sank steadily into the mud. Finding themselves trapped, the cattle foundered weakly about and shortly resigned themselves to their fate unless a cowhand wandered by to haul them out. Many were lost in smallish mud-holes or found dead in a gulch but two or three feet in width, or in the quicksand of a creek so narrow that it could almost be jumped.

The worst of these, as Johnny Crowheart soon discovered, were alkali holes, where the water oozed out through the thick clay, and which clung to any animal with a ropy tenacity.

"Up here we call it a rope, Crowheart," chided Arty Lamar in response to Crowheart's calling the coiled rope he held a lasso.

"Guess I've a heap to learn about the way of it up here."

Hoarfrost thick as buttermilk puffing out of his mouth, Lamar, at twenty-five perhaps two years older than Crowheart, studied the latest of some dozen cowpunchers just hired on at the Hashknife. He saw another displaced Southerner.

Johnny Crowheart, brimmed hat tugged low over his forehead to help ward off the chill of this spring day edging toward nightfall, hunkered into an old sheepskin, patched Levis and worn brown boots, the coiled rope dangling from one hand, and armed as the other waddy was with handgun and booted rifle, had in his eyes a blued wariness. With those long arms and legs dangling below the rounded belly of his cowpony, he showed the promise of someday being a large man, but his lifestyle, that of wandering cowhand, had both leaned Johnny Crowheart and given him a guarded outlook as to the friendship of Arty Lamar and these new surroundings.

At the approach of the horsemen, a longhorn tried surging weakly out of a bog hole but only succeeded in sinking deeper into the unresisting clay, with its frantic bellowing causing Johnny Crowheart's bronc to jump skittishly sideways while fighting the bit. All of the Hashknife horses were rough-broken, in that a hired bronc buster merely broke them to the saddle and left the rudiments of turning it into a roping horse to the waddy. The hammerhead ridden by Crowheart was one of seven in his string, and he quieted it down with some soothing words as Arty Lamar brought his bronc around the muddied fringes of the bog hole.

Lamar's rope whistled out to loop around the curving horns of the longhorn a good wagon span apart, and quickly he wrapped the end he held around his saddle horn; then he urged his horse forward to take up the slack in the rope. The touch of the rope brought more lowing from the steer and curses from the man trying to free it.

"Crowheart," he called out, "reckon you'll have to rope one of its legs or we'll never get this dumb critter out."

"That'll take some doing since its legs are stuck in that bog hole."

"Afraid of a little mud, Crowheart?"

With some reluctance Johnny Crowheart dismounted, and groundhitching his reins, he stepped gingerly onto the fringes of the softer ground already clutching at his boots as Lamar's horse set its weight against the rope and stepped ahead. One of Crowheart's boots slipped out from under him, and he fell backward into ankle-deep mud, which provoked from the other waddy a pleased grin. Scrambling to his feet, he slogged deeper into the bog hole

15

and managed to coil his rope around a foreleg, then Crowheart sought dryer ground and his saddle. Their ropes working together, the Hashknife waddies managed to drag the longhorn out of the bog hole, and immediately upon gaining its feet, the enraged animal charged its rescuers, something they'd anticipated. They wheeled their mounts to either side, angling the ropes to trip up the steer, and after freeing their ropes, Arty Lamar and Crowheart headed away at a fast canter.

"This is worse than shoveling out the horse barn."

"That stuff smells about the same," commented Lamar. "It's nighting; what say we mosey in."

"Suits me," said Johnny, as he pulled up, slid to the ground, and began stomping his boots on a flat rock to dislodge some of the clinging mud. "Can't seem to get used to this place."

"For certain the Badlands are plumb different. Once the ground thaws out our work'll really pick up. Which means we won't be gettin' much shut-eye."

They were north of the Little Missouri River, where it gorged to the east, and surrounded by a tangled chaos of canyonlike valleys, winding gullies and wash-outs with abrupt, unbroken sides. Now Johnny Crowheart gazed distantly at an isolated sandstone peak, which in the warming days to come would have its soily mixture of gumbo clay and scoria become an eely glue up which no horseman would dare climb, and beyond the peak to a chain of reddish hills lined with blackish layers of lignite whose ridges ended in a sheer cliff.

Climbing into the saddle and following after Lamar, he figured it wouldn't take but one or two wrong turns to get a man lost. The bunkhouse stories had been of cowpunchers simply disappearing out here. Their segundo, Bill Lowman, stated a horseman needed mountaineering skills to pass through these steep and broken buttes, and told of an outfit trying to take a shortcut through the Badlands, making only four miles in three days with its wagons before turning back.

But young Crowheart, despite his misgivings about this place, had to admit there was a certain quiet majesty in the way the setting sun set to shimmering the layered ribbons of colored rock: gray, coral, red and the shades of brown and black. The heavy spring air had brought out the scents of newborn vegetation, and of rocks smelling of damp mold, with the unexpected appearance from time to time of bighorn sheep, elk, mule or whitetail deer. There was considerable snow melt, with rivulets of water seeping down from higher up and gleaming dully in the diminishing light of day. Gorging a hundred mile track through these sunken mountains was the Little Missouri River and lesser tributaries, the sustainers of life for the longhorn and wild horse and others calling this home.

Snuggling deeper into his sheepskin, Johnny felt more keenly the bite of the northerly wind riffling at his muddy clothing. And he didn't look forward to the five mile or so ride back to the main buildings. There was still a lot of snow, but in scattered patches, embedded with loamy soil that streaked it, and small pebbles thrown there by the wind. Distantly, off to the southeast, a column of smoke marked the site of a burning coal vein, set aflame by errant lightning or brush fires.

To keep his mind off the growing chill as he loped alongside Arty Lamar, Johnny pushed his thoughts southward to about a month ago when he'd hired on with the Hashknife, that being down at Medora, so named for the wife of its founder, the Marquis de Mores, a transplanted Frenchman. At the time he'd been nursing a warm stein of beer while gazing ruefully at his life savings: six bits winking dully under lamplight spilling down upon the crowded bar in the Plainsman Saloon.

Ever since a carpetbagger had sat down before the piano to play a medley of tunes, going on a half-hour now, Johnny had been eying a black-bordered notice tacked among others up along the back bar, the gilt-edged words in it telling that workers were needed over at the local meat packing plant owned by the Marquis de Mores. This, and other local lore, had been detailed to him by an out-of-work cowpuncher he'd been buying drinks for.

"That'd be awful bloody work."

Squinting at his empty beer stein, the waddy said to Crowheart, "I reckon so. My feet couldn't stand being out of the saddle for any length of time. We're lucky though."

"How's that?"

"Coming onto spring. Saw some ranchers checking into the Rough Rider Hotel; here to hire waddies such as us."

"That would suit me right down to the hole in my left boot." He rapped a quarter against the bar to get the barkeep's attention—and for his efforts drew an angry glare from a buffalo hunter with his elbows hooked on the front end of the bar. Crowheart was sort of mellowed out from all the drinking he'd done. And trouble to him was the realization he'd soon be dead broke, the occasional hunger pang gnawing at his belly reminding him of that, and that just maybe he should head over to the Cowboy Cafe for another helping of steak and eggs and sour cream biscuits.

"You're awful loud!"

"My humble apologies," Crowheart called out to the buffalo hunter, then yelled to the barkeep, "What the heck, let's splurge—two fingers apiece of Four Roses . . . and refill our beer glasses." Broke now, but still somewhat clear-headed, he received from his drinking companion a grateful smile.

"Mr. Crowheart, suh, I do admire your hospitality."

"My pleasure, Mr. Walton," said Johnny, and then his attention was caught by a hunting knife that pierced lamplight and sliced at a finger of his right hand reaching to shove the change toward the barkeep. The knife quivered in the stained bar top.

"Company."

"Yeah," muttered Johnny.

"He's sure big."

"Kind of lardy, though. A regular pain in—"

"I get your drift." Stepping away from the bar as did Johnny Crowheart, the waddy added, "Long time since I've seen Yakima Pierce."

"You're acquainted?"

"Somewhat."

"What's that supposed to mean?"

"Over at Miles City he claimed I cheated him out of fifty bucks in a friendly poker game."

"Then why's he gunnin' for me?"

"Drunk as Yakima is, he probably mistook you for

me. Wants your dinero and a piece of your hide."

"Won't get much of either," Johnny mumbled worriedly as he wiped the blood seeping from his cut finger onto his Levis.

Back in a cramped area between the poker tables and three connecting booths, a black potbellied stove threw off shimmering heat waves to bring out the pungent odors of stale beer, whiskey slop and tobacco smoke to prick at the nostrils of those in the saloon. There were other unsavory odors too, such as that reeking from the buffalo hunter Yakima Pierce, a wide blocky man equal in height to Crowheart, but of craggy bearded countenance. Pierce's unshapely hat was grease-stained as was the clothing showing under the long buffalo-hide coat, and where his shirt lay open on his breastbone, the flannel underwear he wore next to his skin was more a grimy black than grey.

Yakima Pierce reached over and retrieved his hunting knife along with Crowheart's six bits, then he spat out drunkenly, "Cowpoke, you're stinkin' up my air!"

If anything, Crowheart mused before responding to the insult; this miserable buffalo hunter had contaminated with his presence this waterhole otherwise knows as the Plainsman Saloon. So's it was time to set the record straight, a reckless notion spurred on by his somewhat alcoholic state of the moment.

"I'll bet your friends—that is if you've got any—call you porker!" That was uttered with the placating manner of a Baptist preacher sorrowing over a dearly departed member of his congregation.

This evoked from Ike Walton a pleased grin and these words: "Mr. Crowheart, suh, I think you've got

Yakima's undivided attention."

Mouthing curses, the buffalo hunter came at Crowheart with that wicked hunting knife flailing away. Somehow, Crowheart evaded the knife before he managed to kick the weapon out of the buffalo hunter's hand. Then they were grappling, with Yakima Pierce clawing at Crowheart's face and drawing blood. When they fell apart, a roundhouse right sent Crowheart reeling backward toward one of the front windows ornately decorated with frames of glass imported from Chicago. Yakima Pierce followed up with another hard blow that sent the luckless cowpoke through the window to shatter it and come down hard on his back outside on the fringe of boardwalk.

In the saloon, Ike Walton stepped forward when the buffalo hunter brushed the front of his coat aside and pulled out a big Dragoon revolver. Unleathering his .45 Peacemaker, Walton brought the butt of it cracking across the back of Yakima's head, and the man slumped into sawdust.

Shaking his head to clear it, Johnny Crowheart got his first glimpse of the man he'd come to call bossman, Jake Murdock, standing alongside his segundo, Bill Lowman; both ranchmen wore amused grins. A shift of Crowheart's head the opposite way revealed slim legs tucked into Levis and high-heeled boots. A further elevation of his pain-squinting eyes showed a Levi jacket and silky red bandanna, with the few shards of sunlight still left tinting the flowing raven hair spilling onto slender shoulders. The hair framed an exquisitely beautiful face, which wore a frown for Crowheart, but all he could do under the impact of the woman's dark amber eyes was smile before one of the men behind her sneered:

"Seems that punk kid can't fight either."

And that was how Johnny Crowheart first came to set eyes upon Carrie Morgan, who he would eventually discover lived with her father and three brothers up north of the Hashknife in the general vicinity of Caprock Coulee.

Johnny Crowheart's bronc slipping as it came off a rise brought him back to the cold reality of the present. Though he blinked away the remembrance of Carrie Morgan, that first and only view of her had set him to thinking that just maybe he'd stick around these Badlands for a spell. Ike Walton, his erstwhile drinking partner back at Medora, had also hired on with the Hashknife, along with filling Crowheart in on the pedigree of the Morgan clan—claim-jumpers and worse, according to Walton.

The spark of sunlight westward ebbed away leaving the Hashknife waddies with another two miles to go, and now Lamar's upthrust hand caused them both to rein up. He pointed ahead to a lower reach of ground running along Squaw Creek, and worriedly said:

"Ground's chewed up."

What Arty Lamar had spotted was an old buffalo wallow, a place along the creek which buffalo had formed by rolling on their backs and sides in an attempt to coat their hides with mud to lessen the sting of summery mosquitoes. The buffalo wallow had, over a span of time, filled up and been covered with a sun-baked crust to match the surrounding terrain. But if a longhorn or horseman came along and rode unwarily over it, he'd sink into the wallow as if he had stepped on a trapdoor and, if not found in time, would perish in the gripping throes of the bottomless mud. This was Lamar's fear as he rode on cautiously.

"Getting too dark to pick up sign of what happened," Lamar said.

"Arty, seems to be some tracks off to our left; cattle, I think."

"Something probably spooked them."

Arriving near the buffalo wallow, they squinted down while trying to catch any sign of a longhorn which might have blundered in, and then Crowheart reached over and touched Lamar's arm.

"Appears that someone's hat is caught in that clump of bushes." Sliding to the ground, Crowheart went over and retrieved the hat. When he walked back to the horses, Lamar struck a flame to a match, while Crowheart murmured wonderingly, "Ain't this Jamison's hat?"

"It be his alright."

"What now?"

"Just make certain we don't get caught in there," he said bitterly. "But it could be, though, he just couldn't find it."

"Doesn't seem likely."

"Nope." Lamar agreed, "it doesn't seem likely a-tall."

Angling away from Squaw Creek to higher and safer ground, they cantered silently ranchward. Stars were beginning to flutter like spring flowers enticingly opening their vari-colored petals with the wind still a constant force. In Crowheart's mind rang the tales passed on to him back at the bunkhouse of others simply vanishing out here. Now it would be their turn—that is, if waddy Jamison wasn't back there—to add to the deadly lore of these Badlands. He felt drained, empty in both belly and mind; he had aged a little, too. And the feeling he was shaking some from the increasing cold of early night didn't strike Johnny Crowheart until they came around a low bluff and upon welcoming ranch lights guiding them toward the flood plain of the Little Missouri.

The Hashknife buildings were actually strung on higher ground northeast of where Squaw Creek poured its copper-colored waters into the river. Both the creek and Little Missouri wended in diamond-back fashion between chains of high bluffs and through small valleys with wooded bottoms. Oftentimes the entrance of a coulee slashed down between abrupt cliffs to the river valleys. Decked out in front of the main ranchhouse to shelter it from wintry storms and the heat of summer were cottonwoods, swayed now by the moaning wind. Paths had been chopped through thorny underbrush and trampled by cattle. In the evenings the men of the Hashknife would idle around the bunkhouse or on the front porch of the main house and watch deer come timidly out of hiding to seek river water. The other buildings, the stable, sheds, bunkhouse, were of log construction and chinked with moss and mud. Pens for the cattle were brought in during the winter, and there were two corrals: a large one to hold horses kept during the day, and a smaller roping corral, with a snubbing post in its center and a wing strung out along one side of the gate entrance, for the saddle band to be driven in without undo difficulty. There was a large garden, just under an acre in size, first tended by the rancher and now under the care of the cook, Woody Hannagan, long ago a better than average working hand, and the Lopez's, a Mex couple the rancher had brought up with him from Texas.

Other cowpunchers were down at the corrals when Lamar and Crowheart rode past the main house and halted their tired mounts. As Arty Lamar slid to the ground, Bill Lowman poked his head out of the tack shed, and Lamar went over there and handed to Lowman the hat found by Crowheart.

"Jamison's."

"Where'd you find it, Arty?"

"Near a bog hole up north along Squaw Creek."

"Well, Jamison and that bunch aren't in yet."

"That buffalo wallow was really stirred up. All we found were the hat and some tracks left by cattle."

"Fresh?"

"Appear to be."

"Howdy, Crowheart. Anything to add to this?"

"Nossir."

"Okay," said a troubled Bill Lowman. "Tend to your horses, then chow up." He began turning away, then swung back and said to Crowheart, "Seems you got baptized in that mud, too."

"Just learning the ropes" came back Johnny's reply. Through the concern he felt for the missing waddy, part of the lonely feeling he'd been carrying around since coming to the Hashknife went away as he returned the segundo's smile, and somewhat more light-footed he began unsaddling his horse.

Bolder winked the stars as the night wore on, but slowly, with everyone at the Hashknife waiting for the remaining hands to come in. After a change of clothes, Crowheart had supped and would have sought his bunk, but the worry of wondering about Jamison kept him up. While the others in the bunkhouse sat around the stove partaking in small talk, four waddies got involved in a pinochle game, cutthroat and no one partners.

"We had orders to pair up."

"Yeah, but Jamison always did like to head out on his lonesome at times."

"As I recollect, he did. Keep that match lit, Arty."

A short time later a shout from outside emptied the bunkhouse, with one of the men who'd been keeping watch pointing northward at some riders loping toward the buildings. Clattering in, one of the horsemen inquired as to whether or not Jamison had returned.

Jake Murdock strode closer to his men and said quietly, "Something like this was ordained to happen, men. The bottom line out here is that reckless men don't last long. So's from here on in, no straying apart. There's a possibility his horse might have gotten away. But if Jamison's in that bog hole, he's in it for eternity; time permitting, men, we'll say a prayer for him up there. Getting tarnable late . . . and with this warm weather starting to move down from Canady, there's a lot of hard days ahead. G'night."

As the men began dispersing, a quiet word from the segundo brought Johnny Crowheart after the man and to a crumbly piece of land overlooking the Little Missouri glinting under starlight. Bill Lowman took his own sweet time about forming a cigarette and lighting it, which set Crowheart's eyes to the sky, and trailing after a shooting star before it winked out.

"Things like this happen, Johnny."

"So I'm learning."

"And there's no time to try and get the body out. Again, maybe it's for the best Jamison stay buried up there; 'cause I'm sure that'll set well with the Almighty Lord, too. Still want to keep on working here?"

"The chow's good, Mr. Lowman."

"Bill's the handle. Then again, maybe you're not wanting to leave has to do with a certain filly living up north of the Hashknife." That was spoken with a teasing smile, but the next sentence from Lowman came out a little harder. "Any paper out on you, Crowheart?"

"My past, Bill, is one of pure recklessness but not stupidity."

"Could be you've just been plumb lucky. . . ."

"That has occurred to me a few times."

"Reckon that pretty much speaks for a lot of us." Trailing cigarette smoke, the segundo paced southward along the high bank, and out from under the cottonwood tree, he stared beyond the river at the sky as a man searching for something in its vastness. In the few years he'd been here, Bill Lowman had leaned more, and the black mane of hair and handlebar mustache had become peppered with grey; but about the Texan was a sureness of movement and eye that a lot of the younger hands envied. When it came to roping or gentle-breaking a horse, the segundo had no equal, and he never bragged about this, though Lowman's reputation as a practical joker was well established around the Badlands. That woman down in Texas he'd been pining after had, after mailing off a letter to the segundo, married an established rancher. He had

27

learned to live with that, as he had come to terms with the ways and moods of rancher Jake Murdock, and this concern for his boss was the reason he'd called Crowheart out here. He began explaining this by drawling, "Jake's only kin is due home soon. Darin Murdock's kind of spoiled. Been back east at college—that is, until he got kicked out, or so his pa said. Makes no sense Darin coming back here."

"Why's that?"

"Hates ranchin' and his pa among other things. He's around your age, Johnny. Reckless though . . . gets boozed up a lot . . . and sure likes his women." He ambled farther along the ledge as the warming weather brought up from the river the croaking of frogs and, from across it, the lowing of cattle settling in for the night. "So why am I telling you this? Well, Crowheart, there's an off-chance you can help me out. I recollect you saying on our way up here from Medora that you'd had some book learning."

"I can read and write some, if that's what you mean."

"The bossman can't," Lowman said flatly. "And not a word about this to the other hands or you'll get your walkin' papers, pronto. You savvy that?"

"Won't breathe a word," he said quickly.

Nodding around the smoke curling up past his eyes, Lowman said, "The last three or four years, and before his son went to college, Jake took the boy along to these spring meetings held by the Stockman's Association. Down in Medora the bossman would have to hobnob with educated folks such as Teddy Roosevelt and that Marquis fella. Since Jake couldn't read or write, it was the boy's chore to take down the minutes of the meeting and other such information."

"Since Jake's son is coming back," pondered Crowheart, "won't he be doing the same thing this year?"

"After what happened to Darin Murdock back at college, I'd say not. Seems he got into trouble with the law; him and a couple of others got caught robbing a jewelry store. Jake's influence and money got his son off with a stiff fine while the others were sent to jail. The other condition was that Darin Murdock come back here and pick up some slack. Plainly stated, Crowheart, I feel the boy is going to wind up with that drinking crowd of his again—or worse."

"So the gist of all this, Bill, is that you want me to perform that chore—"

"Yup, but I'll have to talk Jake into it. Ramrodding the Hashknife is too big a job or I'd tag along. By the way, where'd you spring from?"

"Western Oklahoma until I was fifteen . . . then a lot of other places."

"That pretty near makes you a Texan."

"You mind if I pair up with Ike Walton?"

"What's wrong with Arty Lamar?"

"A little too testy for my blood."

"Guess Lamar's got that rep, alright. Walton, huh?"

"Walton owes me for all them drinks I bought down at Medora. Meanin' he can get into them bog holes instead of me."

A rumble of laughter came from Bill Lowman as they cut back toward the bunkhouse. With that the segundo said, "It'll give me a lot of pleasure telling old Walton this."

They parted by the bunkhouse, the segundo strolling over to the small log house he called home, and Crowheart going into the darkened bunkhouse and finding his bunk. Despite the tragedy of this long spring day pressing at his thoughts, Johnny Crowheart had only moments to form an image of Carrie Morgan before sleep claimed him.

Chapter Three

A Chinook sweeping out of the Rockies spelled the end of the long winter. This warm, dry wind piercing into the Badlands brought the men of the Hashknife up earlier than usual, which they did anyway well before dawn. Rising before them had been Woody Hannagan and Felipe Lopez to prepare the morning meal, and so from the chuck house came chimney smoke being lined southeasterly by the warming wind.

A crack of a smile came from the dour-faced Hannagan at the Spanish song whistling softly from Felipe Lopez. They had, over the years, gotten broke in to one another; but despite this, Woody Hannagan ruled the chuck house, and he was a more than adequate cook, his speciality being bear sign, sourdough biscuits and a milk gravy that brought many a chuckline rider stopping by for some free grub. Winter or summer would always find Hannagan clad in a red woolen shirt and matching suspenders, the worn bowl of a briar pipe showing in a pocket. A confirmed bachelor, he tolerated cowpokes rather than liking them.

Most of Felipe Lopez's worries of late were for his

wife, Rose. She'd been ailing, a heart condition. They hadn't been blessed with children, and in his late sixties, Lopez knew this had been God's will. They lived over at the main house, where Rose Lopez cooked for the rancher and kept things orderly. Age had stooped Lopez, lined his face as of an oaken tree, and chinked the black hair with whitish streaks.

"Open the oven, Felipe."

Felipe Lopez stopped stirring the hunks of potatoes frying in the pan and bent to open the oven door with the hem of the long apron he wore; then Hannagan slid into the oven a couple of pans of sourdough biscuits. He crossed over and began cutting hunks of slab bacon into thick strips as Lopez said:

"Nunca se sabe lo que puede pasar . . ."

"What can happen? About the weather or what?"

"About young Murdock coming *en casa?*"

"Felipe, the boy's always been a troublemaker. Caused me no end of grief, too. Just don't know."

"Si . . . as he has me. My prayers go out to him . . . and Señor Murdock."

"Suppose that's about all a person can do," Hannagan said curtly, as he placed the strips of bacon into another frying pan warming atop the big cast-iron range. He stepped around Lopez and went into the dining room to light the hanging coal-oil lamps. As Woody Hannagan began cleaning with a wet cloth the long rough-wood and varnished table, his eyes passed along it to where waddy Jamison always used to sit while chowing down. Nearly a week had passed since that tragic incident, the cowpoke's horse having been found a day later wandering along a coulee. Sign found at that bog hole told of how the horse had blundered in and somehow managed to free itself but leaving its rider to die. It was a way of life accepted by the Hashknife waddies. There were other dangers, too, mused Hannagan, cattle stampeding or an occasional firefight with rustlers.

Back in the kitchen, he inquired, "How's it coming, Felipe?"

"Call them in anytime."

"First we'll have us some Arbuckle's." Filling two tin cups with coffee, he brought them over and passed one to Lopez. "If'n we would have stayed down in Texas, Felipe, maybe Murdock's son would have turned out better."

"*Quizas* . . . if the mother would have lived."

Nodding in agreement, Hannagan emptied his cup and said while turning toward the back door, "Chuck away time." Out on the covered back porch, he picked up a metal striker from one of the chairs reposing there and began rattling it against an angle iron, the clanging sound spilling through the lifting darkness to the bunkhouse. As the waddies began piling outside, Hannagan returned to the kitchen and began helping Lopez carry platters of food into the dining room.

The men ate hungrily, without too much small talk, and before the others were finished breakfasting, the dew wrangler, who'd already saddled his horse, left to mount up, hunt up and bring in the saddle band. As a rule, when the horses were turned loose at night, they split up into two or three bands. Always left alone were the mares with their colts, the mares not being ridden by the cowhands due to the trouble caused by them when mixing with the other horses.

While most of the men lingered over coffee as they

waited for the wrangler to arrive with their horses, Johnny Crowheart took his leave from the table and left the chuck house a stride in front of Ike Walton dragging on a cigarette. Throughout the warming days of spring, and even during winter, there had been little snowfall. But this unexpected weather change had already worked havoc with the scattered patches of snow remaining, for dimly in the palish light Johnny could tell that in some places the Little Missouri had overflown its banks as had Squaw Creek; but together both ribbons of water posed no threat to the ranch buildings.

By common accord they moved silently toward the corrals, savoring the warming air. Overhead a night hawk swung away at their approach, to leave a lonely tuft of feather fluttering onto Crowheart's sleeve. He eyed it and the eastern horizon just becoming red-rimmed, and he yawned.

"These hours getting to you?" Walton asked.

"Sure are, Ike. Don't tell anyone"—gingerly he felt along his ribcage—"but I got thrown yesterday."

Walton laughed softly and said, "That a fact, now. You fall asleep in the saddle?"

"I tell you, Ike, it's plumb suicidal working cattle in these parts. Seems it's all up or downslope. Arty Lamar's tough to pard up with . . . bossy as he is."

"For certain Lamar's got a cantankerous side. But I got the word from the ranch foreman about us pairin' up. Don't know, though, as how I want to be paired with some greenhorn can't set his saddle properly."

"Doggonit, Ike, you owe me."

"Just a good bender is all, Johnny boy."

"Been looking for you two renegades," said Bill

34

Lowman as he veered toward them. He undraped from his left shoulder a saddlebag bulging with supplies and handed it to Walton. "You two'll be headquartering out of the Buckhorn line camp for the next few days. This weather'll bring a lot of frost out of the ground. So be careful up there."

"That ain't all this weather'll root out."

"Meaning . . . rustlers? You see any longriders, Ike, make tracks back here. They could also be riders from that grassy sack outfit . . . Ezra Morgan's kin." He glanced at Crowheart. "You just might see that girl up there, too, Johnny, but now's not the time to be socializing, savvy."

"Gotcha, Bill," he replied.

"Heard that her brothers carved up some cowpoke real bad when he came a-sparkin' her. Hope this don't happen to you." He handed Crowheart the other saddlebag.

"Kiyeee!"

The cry of the wrangler bringing in the horses emptied the chuck house, with everyone drifting toward the corrals. This weather change had gotten to the horses, too, for they went past Crowheart at a fast center, nipping at one another and bucking. Though the sky was brightening, it was still dark under the trees where they walked. Once the horse were in the corral and circling warily, a couple of waddies holding coiled ropes crouched inside and moved centerward to the snubbing post, there to eye the horse each wanted. Expertly their ropes snaked out, and in short order they led their horses out of the corral.

In the corral were three horses belonging to Johnny's string, an apron-faced bay, a sorrel, and one he

35

considered his best roping horse, Pearly Gate, its dun-colored coat fading into a smoky tone, and what Lowman called a bayo cebruno. Sensing Crowheart's intentions, the dun veered away from the rope and edged nervously amongst the other horses, trying to avoid a day being saddlebound.

Chuckling, Ike Walton yelled, "Seems you can't rope either, Johnny boy."

Smarting under the amused grins of the others he rode with, Crowheart managed to rope the dun on his third attempt, and once it was out of the corral, it submitted docilely to being saddled. This was merely a ruse, for Johnny knew from painful experience the dun Pearly Gate had a nasty habit of bucking when the man astride it relaxed some in the saddle; but once it cleared its head of that notion, it generally behaved the rest of the day.

Both Crowheart and Ike Walton, as did most of the other hands, used an apple-horn or Texas rig, a saddle using two cinches and easing a man's back with a high cantle. Now Johnny secured the saddlebags behind the cantle and urged his dun after Walton riding away on his claybank, John B. As they rode past the other corral, a horse ridden by waddy Shorty Walsh began bucking and snorting through its nostrils, and Ike Walton swung his horse sideways to face Crowheart and said, "A dinero says Shorty grabs the apple 'cause that grey of his is sure fence worming it."

"You're on."

Both riders drew up as Bill Lowman eased alongside on his cutting horse. "Shorty should know better than to trust that high poler." And when Shorty Walsh's horse suddenly broke into a gallop, Lowman added, "Reckon you just lost another bet, Walton. A man with your track record at gambling should know better. Here comes the bossman."

Walking stiffly along a dusty lane edging away from the main house, the sun just beginning to send orange light stabbing at his back, Jake Murdock grimaced and drawled tangily, "Guess it is too warm to be wearin' this sheepskin at that. But I figured we was about due to have one of these . . . Chinooks."

"Jake," said Lowman, "Walton, and Crowheart here, are heading up to Buckhorn."

"Rough country thereabouts. Make certain you check out all the waterholes. West of you there'll probably be some of the Elkhorn waddies doing the same thing." The rancher was referring to Teddy Roosevelts Elkhorn Ranch. "Could be rustlers up there, too, so keep your eyes peeled."

"Will do, Mr. Murdock."

"Crowheart, my foreman's been trying to con me into taking you along when I go to Medora."

"Yeah . . . yessir, Mr. Murdock, that's what—"

"Thinking on it," the rancher cut in. "Best make tracks, boys, and earn your forty a month and found."

After the waddies had scattered away from the ranch buildings, Bill Lowman voiced his suspicions to the rancher that Ezra Morgan and his sons, sod-bustin' as they were up around Caprock Coulee, might be rustling Hashknife cattle. "If you recall, Jake, I had a little scuffle with Joe Bob Morgan down at Medora last summer. Joe Bob's not the kind to forget something like that."

"I hear Abe and Trace Morgan are just as bad. The

Morgans are small potatoes, Bill; shouldn't be too much trouble runnin' them out of the Badlands. But that ain't my nature. Guess I'll need more than suspicions."

"Suppose you're right."

"What upsets me was running into Yakima Pierce at Medora. That buffalo hunter has sure gone bad."

"And when you see Yakima, Turk Widen and his bunch aren't too far behind."

"Seems to me Widen got arrested over at Billings and was sent to territorial prison. . . ."

"Could be he's still there hammerin' rocks at that, Jake. Along with Widen's gang, there are other outlaws drifting thisaway. What we need bad is a sheriff, or at least a U.S. marshal."

"At least we got a new sky pilot—maybe Reverend Charley Hunt can preach the devil out of these longriders." They shared a quiet smile. "So, Bill, you mentioned this Crowheart kid having the rudiments of learning?"

"So he told me."

"My son's always handled that chore at the spring stockmen's meeting."

"Could be that your son just might not decide to come home."

"He's stubborn, alright . . . and kind of wild. But he's all I've got."

Bill Lowman glanced away from the sudden pain cutting into the rancher's crinkled eyes, along with concealing the deep resentment he felt for Darin Murdock. The boy was more like his ma, laid to rest going on ten years now. After the death of his wife, Jake Murdock buried himself in trying to build up the

Hashknife, had had little time for his son, and now they'd become strangers.

"By the way, did your sending Crowheart up to Buckhorn have anything to do with that Morgan woman?"

He smiled back at the rancher. "Maybe."

"Why, Mr. Lowman, never knew you to play matchmaker before." Now the rancher scratched a thoughtful finger along his jawbone. "Or is this some devious ploy more in line with your true nature . . . ?"

"Guess you caught me cold-handed, Jake. And speaking of nature, seems no one can control it, be it the weather or this gender thing. Sooner or later Crowheart'll run into them Morgans. And from that look in Carrie Morgan's eyes when she first sighted Johnny over at Medora, he'll be more than welcome."

"Does he know this?"

"Like I said, nature'll take its course."

"Meanin' a woman can control that, too."

"Pretty darned much."

"You surprise me, Mr. Lowman, truly you do." He clapped a hand upon Lowman's wide shoulder, and together they began strolling, the segundo's horse stepping behind them and nipping at dewy grass, toward the main house and a snifter or two of Rose Lopez's strong Mex coffee. "Didn't know you was a regular walkin' encyclopedia when it came to women."

"There's this sudden feeling I'm about to get blindsided."

"You don't go into the Oyster Grotto just to palaver with Blood-Raw John everytime we hit town. It's more in the line of settin' your eyes on . . . now, what's her name . . . ?"

"You know dang well what her name is, Mr. Murdock."

"Jo Ann; got a nice ring to it."

"So?"

"Your work's been slippin' of late, Bill. Was me, now, I'd say this woman is fixin' to place her brand on you."

"Come on, Jake, I'm edging' toward rocking chair time."

"That's pure hogwash, my friend. I know, I know, you set a wide loop for that woman down in Texas, and she got away. But just remember this, not too many men are lucky enough to have another go-around at a good woman. But as you said, Bill, women being able to control nature and all, this could just be wishful thinkin' on your part."

"Doggone," said Bill Lowman as he followed the rancher into the kitchen. "Never should have sent Crowheart up there."

Chapter Four

For the better part of three days Crowheart and Ike Walton had been scouting out draws, valley floors and coulees for livestock, which were plentiful, and wearing brands such as Three Sevens, OX, Long X, W Bar, Eaton VI, or the Maltese Cross. The cattle were gaunted, and upon spotting a horseman, a critter that hadn't been around since last fall would walleye before spooking away. Though a few calfs were in evidence, most of the cows were in calf—and there were some dry cows, those not having calfed last year, which were slicker of hair and more rambunctious that the others.

They'd been looking amongst the calfs for sign of hair branding, oftentimes used for trail-branding but practiced up here in the Badlands by outlaws. It was not an uncommon trick to hair brand a calf with the owner's brand, which meant that it escaped the proper branding held in the spring; then, when this hair grew out, the animal would be rebranded by the thief. Among the cattle they also searched for sign of ailments, blackleg, Texas tick, or those having come down with worms. Once in a while they'd come across tracks left by riders meandering across the northern fringes of Hashknife land.

Alone like this, with an occasional joke or snide remark about his abilities as a cowpuncher coming from Ike Walton, Johnny felt more at ease. Their sojourning rides during the lengthening days of spring had given him more insight into this rugged cliff-dwelling land, making him aware of things he'd passed blindly before. Growing from sheer cliffs were gnarled junipers and clumps of brush, their roots making a network of hairline cracks in solid rock so that someday it would crumble. Water had eroded cannonball concretions into bluffs. Here and there the forces of fire from burning coal veins had caused huge rocks to heave and tumble into new and unruly resting places. Now, taking his ease on Pearly Gate on the floor of a coulee they'd been scouting out, he gazed curiously at a petrified log standing upright some thirty feet.

"Long ago, it's claimed, this was a tropical place. That could have been a sequoia tree," Walton said.

"Suppose next you're gonna claim prehistoric animals such as . . . as dinosaurs roamed around here. . . ."

"S'matter of fact, Mr. Crowheart, they did."

"This another of your tall tales, Ike?"

"This I can prove, as I've seen some of them burial places; saw bones there bigger'n you, Crowheart. Okay, let's drag out thoughts ahead a few thousand years to these tracks." Passing along a barren creek bed were shod hoof markings left by two horses. "Couldn't have been more than a month ago."

"Or made last year during the fall roundup."

"Nope," Walton said flatly. "Whoever it was came through this spring. Maybe that wolfer, Ezra Morgan." A nudge of his left spur sent the claybank northwesterly at a walk.

Though the Chinook had spent its warming fury within a day's span, the warm weather had continued; today it was in the low sixties, a spring day that eased a man's muscles and made him appreciate the coming of summer. Already prairie grass was greening, and buds could be seen on the few trees they encountered. The azure sky was marked with high bands of cloud, whitish and reflecting afternoon sunlight.

Passing through the coulee mouth, they scared up a small band of wild horses sunning themselves on the near bank of a nameless creek, all mares except for a grey stallion. Johnny called out, "I like the cut of that horse."

"Just try catching it." Walton brought his claybank, John B., onto the creek bank and eyed those wild horses cantering to disappear over a distant ridge. Troubling him was this overabundance of wild horses—the fourth band they'd seen up here—and cattle pushing the grasslands beyond their capacity to support them for too much longer because there'd been little rainfall the last two years. Unlike the millions of bison that once roamed the length and breadth of the Great Plains, these beeves munched and trampled the same meadows four seasons of the year. Nor were they cut out for the severe winters for which the buffalo had been well-suited. All it would take, came Walton's unspoken fear, was an early winter marked by a lot of storms.

They crossed the creek, as did those tracks they'd been following, to follow the creek gouging through a shallow ravine and now, according to Walton, to hook up with Squaw Creek. He pointed out a hovering butte and said, "Just beyond that butte you'll find Caprock Coulee" he formed an impish smile—"and that Morgan layout."

They lost sight of Squaw Creek as their horses carried them into thick stands of cedar and willow, and they glimpsed a steer slipping away. Crowheart grimaced at a branch slapping at him, the sting of it sending pain needles dancing along his right shoulder, and he would have sworn that Pearly Gate veered purposely toward another tree just to have its rider suffer more discomfort.

"Knock it off," he muttered as Ike Walton cleared the trees and drew up sharply.

"You hear that?"

"Yeah . . . sounds like someone's in trouble . . . and upstream."

Urging their mounts into a lope, the Hashknife waddies tore through more underbrush to suddenly come out on a slope giving them a view of Squaw Creek and what appeared to be another cowpoke trying to avoid the angry intentions of a cow while out in midstream struggling to free its calf. Spring run-off had deepened the creek, and its swift and treacherous current of chocolaty waters kept the cow from venturing out farther.

When the calf suddenly came free from the gripping quicksand, it lunged forward, plunging itself and the cowpuncher beneath the churning waters. A sudden fear gripping him, Crowheart dismounted at a run that carried him into the creek. At this point Squaw Creek was wide and deep, its waters forcing him into an angling swim. Then the other cowpuncher surfaced to reveal longish black hair clinging wetly to an ashen face. The calf, meanwhile, had been brushed by the current into shallower water and was struggling and lowing toward the cow. Just as Johnny reached out desperately for Carrie Morgan as she was being swept away, Ike Walton's rope splashed across an arm. He grabbed it as well as wrapping an arm around the woman. On the bank, Walton began pulling them toward shoreline.

"That was cutting it close," said Walton, as he helped Johnny carry the woman onto a stretch of grass close to the underbrush. Only after they had set Carrie Morgan down did the waddies notice the blood staining her hair at the left temple.

"Them calves can be ungrateful at times."

"Yeah," agreed Johnny. He glanced anxiously at the sun plunging beneath western rimrocks. "Won't be long before the night chill sets in."

Ike Walton went down the bank and reached to pick up Johnny's hat lodged amongst some reeds, and coming back, he said, "Don't know how bad she's hurt. But our Buckskin line camp is a lot closer than the Morgan place. Best we get a move on." As both men stared again at the unconscious woman, a deep concern shone in Johnny Crowheart's eyes. He'd never expected to hold Carrie Morgan in his arms, nor even see her up here, but he remembered ranch foreman Lowman's words about him staying away from her place. In a strange way, came this thought, she'd come to him.

Walton chancing to glance at the cow moving angrily away, puzzled over the unfamiliar E Bar M brand on its near flank. Could it be that sodbuster Ezra Morgan had gone into the cattle business? The cow could have been a maverick, but more likely it belonged to the Hashknife, and the waddy began to wonder if those rumors about the Morgan brothers being mixed up with outlaws were true.

"We'd better get her home."

"It's at least a ten mile ride to the Morgan place—by then both of you'll have caught pneumonia."

"Wish I hadn't left my sheepskin back at camp," said Johnny. Donning his hat, he helped Walton carry the woman over to his horse before he placed a boot in the stirrup and climbed into the saddle. The other waddy lifted Carrie up and placed her in Crowheart's arms, and Crowheart reined around and brought his horse at a walk southward along the creek as Walton

46

rode down the woman's horse.

At the shallows edging along the base of a low bluff, Johnny forded the creek, and it was here that Walton loped out front. As he rode, Johnny was all too aware of the woman-scent of Carrie Morgan, of how the wet mass of raven hair felt brushing enticingly against his cheekbone. He'd spent a lot of idle and working moments thinking about her, wondering, too, if Carrie would remember him. No longer did blood seep from her head wound, but she still hadn't come around when they reached the line shack, a half-faced cabin with the south side open to the elements. Right away Ike Walton made a fire in the hay-burner, a round cast-iron stove able to be fueled by wood or hay, and set the coffee pot on it to warm before he tended to the horses.

Crowheart had lowered Carrie Morgan into one of the four bunks in the cabin's only room and placed his sheepskin over her, and when Walton stepped out of the gathering darkness, he said, "No way out of it, Ike, we've got to get her out of those wet clothes."

"Reckon you can handle that."

"Me?"

"How's that cut?"

Johnny turned away from where he'd been facing the bunk and said, "Used water from my canteen to clean it. Isn't too deep; more a bruise than anything."

"Well?"

"Well, what?"

"She'll catch her death of cold you don't get them

47

boots and clothes off of her." A sly grin appeared on Walton's stubbled face. "Isn't love just grand, Johnny boy?"

"Now, Ike, doggonit, I ain't in love with her seein' as how we just met."

"You've been walkin' around walleyed ever since we left Medora. That's love, alright. So get to it."

"Wanna long straw it?"

"Cooking's my specialty, Crowheart. I'll just set about" — Walton swung over and began rummaging through one of the saddlebags — "peelin' me some Mexican strawberries and opening a can or two of dried beef."

"Beans . . . you don't peel beans," groaned Crowheart. "Doggonit, Ike, I . . . I never undraped a woman a-fore. . . ."

"Love's arrow is blind, Johnny boy. Just take your bandanna and cover your eyes. Me. I gotta peel me some beans." Snickering, the waddy set about preparing supper.

"Alright," Johnny muttered, "alright, but I don't want no word of this leakin' back to the ranch."

Although heat coming from the stove was penetrating through his wet clothing, Johnny could still feel the cold of this early spring night. He shucked out of his boots and placed them close to the stove to dry, then somewhat reluctantly he went over and gazed down at Carrie Morgan stirring a little but unaware of what had happened to her. A glance Walton's way showed the waddy engrossed in opening cans with his pocket knife, careful not to look toward the bunk where the woman lay. Quickly, and nervously, Johnny removed her boots, and when he began unbuttoning the heavy flannel shirt, it was with a grateful sigh he discovered under it she had on woolen underwear—under no circumstances would he remove this item of clothing. After he had taken off her shirt and the Levis, there was a brief lingering stare from Johnny for Carrie's full-rounded figure. Then he snugged his sleeping bag around her and finally hung her clothing on the wall close to the stove.

"Now," Walton said smugly, "was that so bad?"

"Guess a man could get used to it." He felt embarrassed saying that, and warmed somehow by the presence of Carrie Morgan.

Maybe a half-hour passed, again an hour, when the steely barrel of a Winchester jabbing at Crowheart's ribcage popped his eyes open.

Levering a shell into the breech, Carrie Morgan shouted, "You scurvy cowpoke! You undressed me!"

"I . . . we . . . we pulled you out of that creek. . . ."

"That's a fact, ma'am."

She spun to bring the Winchester bearing on Ike Walton, and then Carrie said angrily, "Should have known there'd be two of you . . . cowpokes."

"Ol' Johnny there risked life and limb to rescue you."

"Where in tarnation am I?"

"Buckhorn line camp," Walton answered.

"Meanin' you're Hashknife men," she said distastefully.

Vague light filtering from the cherry-glowing stove outlined Carrie's lissome figure to the waddies and dusted palely her oval face and longish hair spilling around her shoulders. She wore only the heavy winter underwear and her anger, then suddenly realized that perhaps these cowpokes were telling her true. Her eyes going back to Crowheart, she remembered that impish smile on his face after he came spilling out of that saloon window and glanced her way. About him there had been a certain elegance.

Afterward, on the long ride back to Caprock, she recalled the opinions of her brothers regarding the man she was staring at now, with her eyes still seething in anger. Joe Bob, Trace and Abe were of the shared opinion that waddy Crowheart was no better'n a hunk of dog meat for getting bested in that bare-knuckle brawl. And as usual, on the way home, Ezra Morgan had remained tightlipped and staring off distantly into a private world all his own. Sometimes her pa could be downright cruel with his offspring. The beatings had ceased when her brothers outgrew their pa considerably. But she knew that her pa was haunted by the past, in that she would run away as had her mother so many years ago. The only people her own age she saw, besides her brothers, out at the homestead were the few outlaws passing through, men even more contemptuous, to her way of thinking, than cowpokes.

"Well, ma'am," said Ike Walton, "we was just being neighborly."

The impact of a rifle slug punched a hole in the stove pipe before slapping into the north wall brought Carrie Morgan spinning around and the waddies bolt upright. Gouging a hunk out of the darkness came the reverberating echo of a Henry.

"Daughter!"

"That's my pa?"

"You in there?"

"I'm here, Pa!"

During this exchange the stove pipe unhinged and toppled to the hard-packed dirt floor, and sparks and soot filled the air. Crowheart made a grab for his holstered gun laying on the floor, only to drop the weapon when Ezra Morgan and his three sons shouldered into the cabin. "Light that lantern," Ezra told Trace Morgan.

"This ain't what you think, Pa."

"Hush your lyin' mouth, woman," said Ezra Morgan as lantern light spilled upon his daughter. "Look at you! Shameless, I'd say. Don't matter which one of these men had you . . . both of them are goin' down."

"They saved my life, Pa," she said desperately, "back at that creek."

"Hush up and get dressed." Ezra Morgan was a bowed and gaunt man, the dark eyes above the full greying beard gleamed with malice and hate. His coat

51

was a couple of wolf pelts sewn together.

"We gonna hang 'em, Pa?"

"More likely cut 'em to ribbons first."

A frightened Johnny Crowheart glanced at the big hunting knife hanging from Ezra Morgan's waist and over at Joe Bob looking a trifle shabbier than he'd been down at Medora. Joe Bob was around six feet, scrawny with scraggly hair bouncing around his shoulders, and more dark-complexioned than his brothers. He carried a Sharps, as did brother Abe, while Trace Morgan had an old Le Mat revolving rifled carbine, which went out of production shortly after the Civil War. All of the Morgan brothers had on faded corduroy trousers and heavy winter coats. Their hats shaded eyes lusting with the need to draw blood.

"Don't matter if we do the job here or out there," muttered Ezra.

Ike Walton got out of his bunk and said carefully, "Your daughter is telling the truth. That cut at her forehead was caused by a calf getting the best of her out in that creek. Knocked her plumb out. We had no choice but to bring her here."

"Would it be otherwise if she wasn't holding my rifle," said Johnny.

"Probably needed it to keep you away from her," jeered Abe Morgan, as he brought the barrel of his rifle clubbing at Crowheart's head. As Crowheart reeled toward the stove, Joe Bob joined in, clubbing away with the butt of his Sharps to spill the luckless waddy to the floor.

"No!" That defiant cry ripping out of Carrie Morgan swung the eyes of everyone upon her. Only Joe Bob suddenly gaped in fear when a slug from the Winchester she held tore his hat away. "Drop those rifles! You, too, Pa!"

"Are you crazy, woman?"

"Do it, Pa, or the next time I'll draw blood! As you and my brothers want to do! It happened like Walton told you. These cowpokes saved my hide."

"You . . . certain?" asked Trace.

"One thing I don't do is lie, Trace Morgan. Now the lot of you, git!"

"And . . . and leave you here with them," yelled Ezra Morgan.

"Yup, Pa, but I'll be along shortly. Now, make tracks with your sons."

A reluctant Ezra Morgan, after letting his embittered eyes sweep chillingly over the Hashknife waddies, followed his sons out into the night. Ike Walton framed a tentative smile as he went over and gazed down at Crowheart shaking his head and struggling to rise.

"Reckon you'll live, pardner."

"Yeah, Ike, thanks to Carrie. I'll say this, though, you've got some mean brothers."

"They are that," she agreed.

"Got a hunch," said Walton, "this won't be the last we'll see of them."

"Probably not," she said. Leaning the Winchester

53

against a wall, she slipped into her clothing, then turned to face Crowheart. "I'll be leaving now."

"But it won't be first light for a good three hours . . . ma'am."

"Pa'll be waiting."

"You sound . . . afraid of him. . . ."

"He's . . . well, temperamental." Now her eyes held Crowheart's, seeming to search into their bluish depths in an attempt to discover just what kind of man he was. That first and brief encounter down at Medora had kindled a spark of interest, and now to Carrie Morgan's intense surprise a muted voice told her that someday this cowpoke would become a part of her life. Always before she'd shied away from even talking to drifting waddies such as Johnny Crowheart. But was she any different, or her family, in that all of their lives they'd been restless drifters, always searching for something that Ezra Morgan couldn't quite get a handle on? She'd grown weary of existing like this. Their homestead at Caprock Coulee wasn't much, more of a prison than anything, but it was a starting point, a place to hang one's hat, which was good enough for Carrie Morgan. Only her pa didn't seem to realize that, rambling on as he'd been doing lately of pulling up stakes and making a try at Oregon.

"You did save my life, Johnny. Thanks . . . and you, too, Walton."

"My pleasure." Brushing a lock of hair out of his eyes, Walton added, "It don't seem right and proper you rushin' off like this. Why, Miss Morgan, I was just fixin' to mend that stove and then rustle up some coffee and vittles. It goes against my grain sendin' a pretty gal away hungry — and in the middle of the night to boot."

"Please, just until first light," Johnny added.

Shaping a soft smile for Johnny, she murmured, "Perhaps that would rile my pa up some. And perhaps I've misjudged you . . . cowpokes, too. . . ."

Chapter Five

Where the Yellowstone River curled eastward toward Blue Mountain, an outlaw named Turk Widen stared bitterly at the empty strongbox taken from the Wells Fargo coach. Two employees of the stageline lay dead, one from Widen's Navy Colt, and with two other outlaws taking credit for gunning down the man riding shotgun.

Nine days ago, Turk Widen had escaped from the territorial prison—but not before hacking a guard to death. His flight had taken Widen beyond Big Snow Mountain and over to Judith Gap to hole up at Mack Blackthorn's small ranch. Then through the outlaw grapevine had come word from Yakima Pierce that a lot of easy money could be made in the Badlands. Two other members of the gang were already at the ranch: hardcase George Ramshorn and one new to the game, Odie Blaine. Another member of the gang was being held at the Musselshell jail, and needing some ready cash, Turk Widen headed that way. Though the outlaws did get Kelly Bartow out of jail, they failed in their attempt to rob the First Mercantile Bank, fleeing in a hail of gunfire and the curses of Turk Widen.

When completely sober, one could never find a more congenial man than Turk Widen—some even compared him to the popular Butch Cassidy. A lot of cattle-town women shared in this opinion, since Widen had a flair about him, being somewhat tall and darkly handsome. He took pride in his appearance, liking to wear a cattleman's leather coat and silken bandannas, generally dark blue in color. He'd thinned out while serving time, and somehow it enhanced Widen's angular face and even rows of bony teeth often framing an engaging smile underneath the trimmed mustache. He wore the one gun, strapped high at his right hip. But make no mistake about it, as a few had done, in that Turk Widen was a cold-blooded killer. Though it was said that another member of the gang, Blackthorn, was faster on the draw.

High-grade alcohol changed Widen, bringing out a sullen streak that became uglier with every shot of whiskey he downed. Which had been the case at Musselshell, that bank job bungled because Widen had attracted too much attention at the saloon. They'd been lucky just to get out of town afterward. The trouble was, Widen enjoyed drinking, and womanizing, and killing just a shade better.

"You mean you actually sell these things?" Turk asked.

Turning his angry eyes away from the empty strongbox, Turk Widen looked toward the stagecoach where the only passenger, a carpetbagger, had been thonged to a front wheel. The man who'd spoken, Mack Blackthorn, was holding up a red chemise, and gathered around him were the other outlaws. Blackthorn, a feisty Irishman whose hands were so small they could fit into Mason jars, cut loose with his peculiar cackling laugh. He tossed the chemise to Odie Blaine, then reached into the carpetbagger's inner coat pocket and pulled out a worn calfskin wallet. "How much you got in there?"

"Please, mister, take it and let me go."

"About forty bucks in paper money—and what's this?" Out of the wallet the outlaw removed some crumbling blue backs, money issued by the Confederacy during the Civil War. Blackthorn's eyes stoning over, he hacked spleen into the carpetbagger's face. "You're a damned Reb!"

"Yessuh . . . but that was a long time ago. Please. . . ."

Over the working gear of a cowhand, Mack Blackthorn had on a yellow rain slicker. Though small of stature, he was hellish with either rifle or handgun. Brushing the slicker open, he unleathered the Colt .45, shoved the barrel into the man's mouth and pulled the trigger. Blood and skull splattered against the stagecoach.

Paling, Odie Blaine mumbled shakily, "Lordy, that carpetbagger had no chance a-tall."

"Neither did Blackthorn's pa back at Gettysburg," another outlaw said laconically. "Anyways, Blaine, them Pinkertons look unkindly upon anyone robbin' a Wells Fargo coach. That carpetbagger would'a fingered us for sure."

The death of the carpetbagger seemed to appease Turk Widen; for a sudden grin chased away his anger, and he called out while swinging aboard his horse, "Alright, rattle your hocks."

The other outlaws drifted over and brought their horses out from under a shading cottonwood. They were horses from Blackthorn's ranch: broncs with altered brands. Mack Blackthorn didn't play cards, or hang around town too much, so to amuse himself he rustled horses. He usually drove them north into Canada, then sold the horses for Yankee greenbacks. And the outlaw took a kind of perverse pride in finding out that a mountie out of Ford Macleod was riding one of them.

Blackthorn said, "Yakima said he was to hook up with us at Marmouth."

"I don't like it any better'n you, Mack," said Widen. "Riding in there broke and hungry. Which we ain't gonna do."

"Reckon that means, Turk, we hit the bank at either Baker or Ekalaka."

"I'm for Baker."

"Aw, let's hit both of them."

In the spring a lot of cowpunchers drifted through Marmouth, so the appearance of five more caused no ripple of interest. The peaceful little cow town supplied the needs of the few ranches spread out along the southern fringes of the Badlands. Splitting up as they passed a lonely outhouse, the outlaws rode under cottonwoods and elms shielding them from a shrill southeasterly wind, a spring wind that came out of the Gulf and worked its warming way northward. The buttes and rough terrain also cut the force of the wind.

Turk Widen swung his horse aside when the Deadwood to Medora stagecoach came wheeling off Main Street and went careening to the south. He found the street just vacated by the stagecoach to be two long blocks packed with business places. Parched from the long ride out of Montana, and still not certain if he'd find Yakima Pierce waiting for them, he swore as his horse shied away from a mongrel darting out from between a couple of buildings and clutching in its jaws a hunk of cowhide.

"I'm hungry enough," drawled Mack Blackthorn, "to eat that hide." Watchfully he walked his horse alongside Widen's; for this was new territory to both of them, and the brands of the horses tethered along the street were some they hadn't seen before.

"Didn't spot that bay of Yakima's."

"Could have stabled it," pondered Blackthorn, as he veered down a side street toward a livery stable. "Think them folks back at Ekalaka got a posse together yet?"

"That banker didn't seem to have too many friends." As he dismounted, Turk Widen glanced upward at a wind-swayed cottonwood spreading its branches over the roof of the livery stable. There was a sort of calm manner about this town he liked, a sort of down-home feeling.

That hadn't been the case after they'd ridden into Ekalaka, Montana Territory, around mid-afternoon and come across a rancher and the local banker getting ready to square off out in the street over a foreclosure notice. So all the Widen gang had had to do was saunter through the back door of the bank and help themselves to some unattended cash before the only clerk who'd been gawking out the front door realized he wasn't alone. Having not cut the dust in his throat with whiskey since leaving Musselshell, Turk Widen was in a charitable frame of mind, and he left the clerk, despite objections from Blackthorn, trussed and alive with divesting the Commercial Bank of Ekalaka of its cash flow—a little over five thousand dollars.

On the way down to the rendezvous at Marmouth the outlaws had detoured over to Baker, leaving as quietly as they'd come when Turk Widen had spotted U.S. Marshal Con Tillison and some of his deputies escorting an outlaw known to Widen out of the local jail and through the crowd hemming in the gallows. Another man Turk Widen hated was up on the gallows, checking out its workings: hangman Elias Poe. There was a temptation to bushwhack Marshal Tillison, but sticking around Baker could see Widen coming down with a sudden attack of hemp fever. He wouldn't forget that Tillison had tracked him down after he pulled that bank job over at Bozeman.

Stabling his horse under the sleepy eyes of a hostler too lazy to heave out of a wicker chair, Turk Widen checked out the loads in his sixgun before leaving the livery stable. He was a cautious man. More than once old habits had kept him alive, and he wasn't about to tempt fate by getting sloppy now. Especially in territory new to him.

"What are you thinking?"

Idly he glanced at Mack Blackthorn wiping sweat from the inner band of his hat. "About coming here? That maybe Yakima didn't?"

"He'll show."

"He's dependable."

"Still, something's eatin' at your craw—"

"Hunger pangs, Mack, that's all; some grub and booze'll take the trail dust out of my mouth. But don't worry, I'll go easy with the hard liquor."

"Just what did that prison doctor tell you?"

"If I ain't careful, I can live to be ninety or more."

"I heard otherwise, Turk, about your kidneys goin' bad."

"Let it lay," Widen said bitterly as they strolled onto Main Street and began checking out the three saloons on the north side. That prison doctor had no right to tell him, Widen mused, that one of his kidneys was going bad. This troubled the outlaw more than he cared to admit. "But with a twenty-five-year sentence staring you in the face," the doctor had gone on, "it won't be whiskey that'll kill you, just the aging processes." Widen enjoyed boozing it up, bad kidneys or not, and he clapped Blackthorn on the shoulder and said flippantly, "I feel a good drunk coming up."

"We ought to salt away some of that money, Turk."

"Spending a year in that territorial prison put a crimp in my socializing. I crave me a lot of whiskey."

"Guess you'll never change. Maybe we should hear Yakima out first? Then if the deal sounds sour, head out of here."

"Got a feeling about this place . . . that it'll be good to us." He shot Blackthorn a grin and elbowed into the Western Bar. Nodding at some men gathered around a poker table, Widen sauntered over to the bar and propped a spurred boot on the railing. The grin was still there when the barkeep came out of a back room toting an armful of whiskey bottles which he placed along the back bar. "Afternoon."

"What's your pleasure, gents?"

"Any action going on besaides that poker game in here?"

"Things don't generally pick up steam until sundown around here. Trailing through?"

"Depends."

Mack Blackthorn eyed a bowl of hard-boiled eggs sitting on the bar and said, "How much for an egg?"

"Compliments of the house. Along with the first drink."

"What's the occasion?"

Somberly the barkeep replied, "I married off my last daughter a week ago. Now it's just me and my dogs and no more handouts. Had five of them."

"Daughters, you mean—"

"That being the case," said Blackthorn, "give me a shot of top shelf stuff and a stein of cold beer."

Despite this friendly conversation with the barkeep, Turk Widen retained his watchful attitude. He had spotted no jail, on the way in or along main street and, since Marmouth was on the stagecoach road, figured the town had law of one kind or another. He wasn't the kind, as the barkeep had done, to place all of his eggs in one basket, since he had noticed telegraph poles coming in from the west. By now the sheriff back at Ekalaka must have sent a passel of wires describing him to a T, and maybe Blackthorn had been right about letting that bank clerk live. Or maybe he was doing all this fretting for nothing, and with a gracious wave of his hand, Turk Widen ordered a drink for the house.

After Widen's third drink, the other members of the gang wandered in to report that Marmouth was just what it appeared to be, a small cow town enjoying a balmy spring day. Wary of the outlaw when he was drinking, all of them except Blackthorn went back and started a game of three-handed pinochle.

They had just gotten into the game, Odie Blaine winning the first three hands, when a woman entered the saloon and beelined over to Turk Widen.

She sid quietly, "Yakima sent me."

"That does relieve some of my anxiety. How's that old salt been?"

"Right now he's sleeping off a drunk," she told Widen, and without waiting for him, she hurried out of the place, with a gesture from Widen fetching the other outlaws. Widen caught up with her just as the woman found a side street.

"You're not very hospitable," he said crossly.

Drawing up short and fastening a bold eye upon Turk Widen, she said curtly, "Going on a week now I've wined and dined Yakima and that friend of his — and not a cent to show for it." The shawl covered most of her hair, with the few locks showing a straggly brown. Widen's eyes took in the bold thrust of her bosom under the long brown dress.

He pulled out some money. "How much does he owe you?"

"Forty bucks should cover it."

"Here's forty . . . and another forty to cover some food. You do cook?"

"Alice Hyatt can outcook anybody in this town, Widen. My place is at the end of the street — the last house on the right."

"Under that big oak tree?"

"That's it. I don't have much in the way of liquor . . . so if you and your boys want some — "

"I take it you're a drinking woman?" He handed her another twenty.

"I'm no slut, Mr. Widen." She draped the shawl

over the front of her dress. "All my no-account cowboy of a husband left me after he cashed in his chips were that house and some washed-out dreams. Yakima ain't much, but at least he keeps his word."

As the woman hurried back uptown, Turk Widen brought his men along the quiet street, the thought in him that she was right about Yakima Pierce being a man of his word. The only thing Widen had learned from bitter experience was that Yakima's memory wasn't all that good. With the old buffer hunter it was just a situation of live and let live, for Widen still remembered Yakima Pierce cutting down on a lawman with that big-bored Sharps 50-90, the famous Big Fifty and ultimate in buffalo guns. That big rifle had drilled a hole through that lawman wide enough to drive a span of mules and a freight wagon. And Yakima rarely missed with it. Like Widen, he was a boozer, which was the chief reason the two men got along so well. Since there weren't any buffalo left, Yakima had joined Turk Widen's fraternal organization called longrider. There were other buffalo hunters who'd gone bad, too, men living for the moment and maybe dead the next. It didn't seem to Turk Widen at the moment he was any different, though he had notions to the contrary. But this damnable kidney disease, he figured, meant he had one or two years at the most to make his stake and then strike to where he wasn't known.

At a quiet word from Blackthorn, a man a hair more cautious than Widen, George Ramshorn and Kelly Bartow unlimbered their handguns and passed along the side of the house. Widen made no comment about this as he stepped onto the front porch creaking under the weight of his boots and opened the screen door. The living room was empty; but the snores of Yakima Pierce carried Widen into a bedroom, and he grinned at the buffalo hunter sprawled naked on the only bed. Going into the hallway, he went down it and found the kitchen as Ramshorn and Bartow came in the back door.

"Is Yakima here?"

"In dreamland." He reached past the hand pump for the pail of water. "Where'd you stable your horses?"

"This town's only got two livery stables," Ramshorn said somewhat testily. "But we'll go get them, Turk. You know, you can be damned irritable at times."

"Irritable is what keeps me alive." Grinning, Widen carried the pail, splashing water down the hallway and into the bedroom occupied by Yakima Pierce. He doused the sleeping man with the water and stepped back.

The buffalo hunter growled angrily as he spun and started up from the bed, but caught himself when he recognized the outlaw. The growl changed to laughter, and he bellowed, "About time you got here, Widen. It was mighty nice of them Montana folks to let you out of jail."

"Expected back before sundown," he came back. "And just returning what you did to me over at Miles City when you caught me with that woman."

"Ain't that what friends are for."

"So, Yakima, what's this big money deal?"

"Part of why I brought this yonker in on it."

"Yonker?"

"Must be this cowpoke sacked out in the other bed-

67

room," said Blackthorn from where he stood in the hallway.

"Name's Darin Murdock — ever heard of that Hashknife outfit?"

"Supposed to be one of the biggest spreads out here."

"It be that, Turk. Ranch is owned by a Texan named Jake Murdock; Darin's his only kin."

"You talking of ransom money?"

Rolling out of the bed, Yakima Pierce used the bedspread to dry himself before he donned his clothing, and then he motioned Widen out of the bedroom and into another. There, in a narrow bed, Turk Widen looked first at the tossel-haired son of Jake Murdock and at the rather obese woman he was snuggled against. The room reeked with tobacco smoke and liquor residue. "So he's the son of some rancher?"

"I'm talking of rustling, Turk."

"Now that can be a sorrowful game," he said dubiously.

"Believe me, pardner, I spent a lot of time and money on this venture. There's others involved besides that kid. I tell you, Turk, these Badlands are full of cattle. There's plenty of places to hide them, and what's right about this is there ain't no law out here."

"That a fact?"

"It be."

"I'd rather discuss this over some chow, Yakima. Rustling?"

"More cattle than you ever seen before — and no law to stop us."

"Maybe this game'll work after all."

Chapter Six

The summons back to the ranch for Johnny Crowheart came shortly after he'd received an unexpected visit from Carrie Morgan. At the time, Johnny had been hazing a cow and its calf out of a coulee known to hold quicksand. The cow kept wanting to break back into the brush, but with Johnny letting Pearly Gate have its head, the bronc blocked each backward move of the cow until it gave up and ambled out of the coulee.

"That's some horse."

Johnny dropped a startled gaze upon Carrie Morgan sitting on her horse under a shading elm. There was something about her smile that got to him, and he blushed. She looked vibrantly alive, lovelier, if that could be possible, then when he'd last seen her. He walked his horse under the tree.

"I've been thinking about you . . . a lot." A closer glance showed Johnny the worried set to her face. "Your pa, he didn't take it out on you for not leaving until morning. . . ?"

"Pa got over it. Johnny, it's my brothers I'm worried about."

"They sure wanted our hides."

"They still do. Especially Joe Bob. He's my brother . . . but awful mean. Overheard Trace and him talking about joining some outlaw gang. They mentioned an outlaw — Yakima something?"

"That'll be Yakima Pierce. He just happens to be the man Ike and I had a ruckus with down at Medora."

"Maybe if that hadn't happened we wouldn't have met. I do like you, Crowheart."

"That sets fine with me," he said awkwardly. "But I doubt if your pa would welcome me at your place."

And with a yearning to take her in his arms, Johnny had watched Carrie Morgan ride away. If love meant thinking about one woman most of the time, then he was smitten with it, along with resentment toward her brothers. He could understand her pa having time and age dry him up, as had happened to his own father. For certain Ezra Morgan had raised three hellers, and upon arriving back at the home ranch, Johnny had filled Bill Lowman in on the intentions of Joe Bob, Abe and Trace Morgan.

"Seems that girl saved your bacon."

"She plumb shot Joe Bob's hat right off," he said admiringly.

"That brand Ike Walton spotted — the E Bar M?"

"We figure it to be Morgan's. Anyways, any man has a right to fashion his own brand."

"Just so Ezra Morgan isn't putting that brand on Hashknife cattle. Or those of our neighbors."

Out in the breaking corral, the bronc buster Murdock had hired slipped off a horse he'd just rough broken and let one of the waddies assisting him lead it out of the corral. It was shortly after sunup and still hazy enough so that moisture bowed tree branches and dampened the boots of Lowman and Crowheart, who where taking a shortcut through reedy grass toward the corral. Both waddies nodded politely at Rose Lopez peeling some potatoes out back of the main house. She'd aged a lot, mused Lowman.

"Buenos dias," Lowman said.

"And to you, Señor Bill." She flashed an affectionate smile for the segundo.

When they reached the corral, the bronc buster, Sandy Norton out of Great Falls, took a breather and came over to chat with Lowman. "Broke some that'll make good riding horses. Just what are your plans for that highbinder?"

Bill Lowman studied the big range stallion lonesoming in one of the corrals. They'd caught the stallion only a week ago and its band of mares. The stallion would be useless as a cowpony because of an incurable viciousness as was the case with horses like this, and because stallions had a habit of driving away the ranch mares. They were a breed of horse fearing no beast except a grizzly, had been known to kill a man on foot, and thus Lowman saw no way out of it: The horse must be shot. Just east of the main buildings lay the boneyard, a place in a narrow ravine where dead cattle or horses were hauled. Out on the range, cattle were left where they had died to decay naturally, with the aid of buzzards and coyotes. Though Bill Lowman appreciated the fine lines and clean limbs of the stallion, he just couldn't let the animal go, and also knowing this, the bronc buster asked Lowman how much he wanted for the horse.

"Well, Sandy, speaking for the Hashknife, I'd say . . . twenty-five bucks." His eyes held a speculating glimmer.

"Will you take twenty?"

"Why this sudden interest in that stallion, if I may be so blunt as to ask?"

"I figure I can break that stallion, Bill. Won't have it around my place though. There's this Englishman out there wanting a good stallion to breed his mares." The bronc buster flashed a smug smile. "Just won't tell him about the nasty habits of them stallions, though."

Laughing, Lowman said, "They say a good horse trader has no conscience. A deal, Sandy." Now the segundo stole a glance at the rancher stepping away from the main house, and he pulled Crowheart aside. "Looks, Johnny, like its time to head to Medora. Just remember, Jake's bark is worse than his bite . . . and Jake's got a rough humor, at times. Just don't let on that you know he can't write. Mostly, he's worried about his son not coming home yet."

Since their horses were already saddled for the trail, all the rancher and Crowheart had to do was swing aboard them and head out. The rancher brought them southward across his land until he hooked up with a dusty road Crowheart later found out carried them to the Badlands town of Grassy Butte, which Jake Murdock detoured by cutting to the northwest and back into the deeper recesses of the Badlands. This was shortly before noon. Johnny didn't find out why the rancher kept them saddlebound until late afternoon sunlight began trying to edge under the brims of their hats. Jake Murdock broke his long silence only after they'd forded a little Beicegel Creek and had passed into McKenzie County.

"We'll be nighting at the O'Connor place. You set a horse fairly well, Crowheart."

"Guess Pearly Gate has a nice pace."

"Like cowboying?"

"Some."

"Well, son, to stick with it you'll have to like it more'n some."

"I mean I cotton to it a lot, Mr. Murdock. This country is real different."

"Easy to get lost in." The rancher began pointing out the different buttes, Cedar Top, Buckhorn, Anderson and Black Top. "And I don't know how many creeks feed into the Little Missouri. By now, I suppose, you're acquainted with a few landmarks up north, such as Stony Johnny and Caprock . . . and where them Morgans are homesteading."

"Uh . . . some, sir."

"Was it just happenstance you saving that girl's life?"

"We come up on that creek, and there she was about to drown."

"You wasn't on your way"—through the scowl, laughter danced in Jake Murdock's eyes—"up to see her now, was you?"

"Nossir! Mr. Lowman gave me orders about that, he sure did, sir."

"Crowheart, I get the drift you were going over to pay your devoirs to that Morgan girl; what we Texans called a jimpsecute."

"A . . . a what. . . ?"

73

"Just another way to say old-fashioned courting. Can't say I blame you none, Crowheart, seeing us how she's prettier than most. But watch your hindside next time you feel the urge coming on to see her."

Jake Murdock brought his going-to-meeting horse as he called the canelo around the flank of a bluff and said gruffly, "There's the Turkey Track."

All that revealed itself to Crowheart was the top of a windmill until they passed down a lowering track and came through trees spread out on lower ground, where a collie bounded toward the arrivals. A cowhand, pedaling a grinder on which he was sharpening a knife, ceased long enough to throw the rancher a friendly wave. Easing up at a walk by the main house settling into the lowering shadows of night, Murdock swung to the ground as a side door opened and the rancher and his wife emerged, folks greying into their sixties as was Jake Murdock.

"Figured you'd be stopping by most any time."

"Howdy, Bucky," said Murdock as he passed to Crowheart his reins, then he stepped ahead and pressed his arms gently around Martha O'Connor. "Honey, how many times have I asked you to leave this old fossil and run away with me."

"Oh, Jake, ever since I've known you. My, it's good to see you." She threw an inquisitive glance at Crowheart. "Where's Darin?"

"You know how them college yonkers are." He kissed her roughly on the cheek and then gestured toward the man he'd ridden with. "This bright-eyed yonker is Johnny Crowheart."

"How do, Johnny," said Bucky O'Connor, the long winter of inactivity having given him a slight paunch,

74

which spring riding was now taking away, the warming sun browning a face chiseled by the years spent in the saddle. He came over and shook Crowheart's gloved hand. "Let me give you a hand with stabling those horses."

"I'd admire to do it, sir."

"What I pay him for," said Murdock. "Curry my horse down, then give it some sweet feed." He followed the O'Connors back through the side door as Crowheart headed whistling toward the low-peaked barn. Along the way he couldn't help noticing that the Turkey Track didn't have as many buildings or corrals as the Hashknife. The waddy who'd been sharpening a knife followed Johnny into the barn and took charge of Murdock's horse.

"How are things up at the Hashknife?"

"Tolerable."

"Worked there for a spell. How's Lowman?"

"Still around."

"So you're Crowheart. They call me Haystack . . . for reasons I'd rather not discuss at the moment." Draping the rancher's saddle on a stall wall, he brought the horse into it, with Crowheart going into the next stall. "Was down at Little Misery a short time ago, an' heard some real bad hombres discussing your future at Grogan's Saloon—you and Ike Walton."

"One of them must have been Yakima Pierce."

"It was. Be nobody to mess with."

"Who was he with?"

"Run of the mill hardcases, I reckon. So's when they began eyeballing me, Crowheart, I vacated the premises. They left town ahead of me, Yakima and them hardcases headin' north."

"Thanks, Haystack, but I've learned a long time ago there's no sense trying to please everybody. Just earning a wage is chore enough for me."

"Same here, I reckon." Leaving the barn on their way to the house, the waddy added, "Chief reason I came here is that Mrs. O'Connor ain't stingy when it comes to settin' a fine table."

"I've found that riding with Jake Murdock you don't stop and chow down."

"He has that rep, alright. Might be that your boss-man admires the way Mrs. O'Connor sets a table, too."

After Crowheart and the waddy known as Haystack had washed up out back and gone into the main house, two other men working for the Turkey Track put in an appearance, and then everyone settled around the big round table dominating the living room. The log house had a low roof covered with sod, with the inner log walls varnished so that they shone dully under the cherry glow of coal oil lamps, and with fluffy curtains covering all of the windows. Since there was company, the rancher helped his wife, Martha, bring in platters of hot food. Between them, Johnny couldn't help noticing, there was a deep affection, an awareness of one another one didn't often see in folks married so many years. Somehow this open display of a shared love made the food taste better, and the platters of roast elk, baked potatoes still in their skins, thick brownish gravy seasoned with cloves, and ample supply of fresh milk, a rare commodity at most ranches, was devoured quickly over the murmur of conversation between the two ranchers.

Afterward, Crowheart would have enjoyed going out and chatting with the other hands, but a quiet word from Jake Murdock brought him after the ranchers into a combination office and den, where Bucky O'Connor opened a humidor and offered cigars around.

"Don't smoke," Johnny said.

"My only vice," said O'Connor. "This, and playing an occasional game of poker with Jake and my fellow ranchers." Striking a wooden match against his belt buckle, he lit both cigars, and as Murdock settled into a big rocking chair and made himself comfortable, an ashtray on a stand at his right elbow, O'Connor sat down in the chair behind his desk and swung it to face his guests. "Seems they hung a couple of rustlers over at Wibaux last week."

"Hanging two or three won't do the job."

"There is talk of a vigilante committee."

"Such an endeavor, Bucky, is for places having fairsized towns and some semblance of law — we have neither. All we need to do when coming against rustlers is form a hanging party right there and get the job done. A few rustlers stretching rope around these parts will get the word out."

"You're right, Jake."

The talk between the ranchers went on, of rustlers and spring roundup, and slowly it dawned on Johnny Crowheart that, in a way, the man he worked for was lecturing to him, telling him the way of it out here in the Badlands. Through the cigar smoke filming around the hanging lamp and the clinking sound as

O'Connor refilled from time to time their small glasses from a bottle of imported brandy, the ranchers instilled in Johnny Crowheart just what this place was all about.

A traveler, upon first viewing the Badlands and stark plains of this Upper Missouri country from a stagecoach or window of a Northern Pacific passenger car, would scarcely believe he was in the middle of a vast grazing country. For he would only see small numbers of cattle or one grazing alone. Little did the traveler comprehend that each cow must have at least twenty-five acres of grazing land. The three sustainers of life for a ranch, which the Badlands had in abundance, were water, grass and shelter. Cattle, it had been proven to the sorrow of a lot of ranchers, would not live through the winter in the foothills of high mountains. Nor out on the open prairie, where even though there might be lush grass, the deep snow and arctic winds would kill off any herd.

"Which boils down to this," said Jake Murdock, as their host refilled his and Crowheart's brandy glasses, "that the present danger we are facing is overstocking."

"Some eastern outfits are bringing in more cattle," agreed O'Connor. "Though Teddy Roosevelt chairs our stockmen's association, it takes more than one man to keep things under control. I'm afraid one bad winter can wipe a lot of us out. Look what happened to that herd of pilgrims over on the Powder River."

Rancher Bucky O'Connor was referring to those cattle driven up from the south, a herd of cattle called "pilgrims," which arrived over on Montana's Powder River during the fall of the year and in poor condition. As the winter of 1880 was a hard one, even for cattle accustomed to snow and cold times, the heavy snowfall of that year saw three-fourths of that herd of around four thousand perishing.

"That was pretty much open range country though," O'Connor went on.

"I'll try to drive this point home," said Murdock.

"Truly I'd like to go down to Medora with you, Jake. Give some of them over-ambitious ranchers a piece of my mind. But that wouldn't be neighborly either, I reckon."

"Martha and this spread wouldn't miss you for a few days. The trouble with you, Bucky, is that you aren't carrying your fair share of the load. Just sending one of your men down to represent the Turkey Track, as you've done for the past two years, I might remind you, isn't of too much help when I have to jaw with them big cattle barons."

"Never considered that before. Or that I really haven't been backing you up, Jake. I could reconsider."

"You do that."

"Crowheart," the man he worked for said so suddenly to the waddy that he almost dropped the small carving of an elk he'd just picked up from the desk, "the meat of why I had you sit in with us old fossils was to sort of fill up that empty space between your ears. Down at them meetings in Medora you'll be my ledger writer. Meaning you'll need to have some inkling of what's going on."

"Yup, it's sure been an earfull."

"Doggonit, Bucky, how many times have you refilled Crowheart's glass?"

"Not close to what you've had, Jake."

"I should hope not," said Murdock.

Much to his surprise, Johnny saw the hands on the windup clock registering five minutes short of eleven. He'd enjoyed himself; another surprise. And this had been a night during which he'd gotten to know Jake Murdock as something more than a cattleman. Out at the ranch, the men considered Jake Murdock a hard taskmaster. Johnny could see now that the rancher had a warm, compassionate side despite the gruff mannerisms. There was Murdock's worry over his son, along with running seven thousand cattle on his ranch.

O'Connor and Murdock had also discussed how the dry summers of the last two years had thinned out the prairie grass. There was little need to cut the grass and let it cure into hay since this lush grass cured on the stalk, banking its nutritional value for winter grazing on the sheltered Badlands ranges. This manner of feeding their cattle worked during open winters, such as they had been having. Hesitantly the young waddy said, "Suppose we get a bad winter?"

"Since I've been here that hasn't happened," said O'Connor.

"We've been shaking dice with these winters and coming up sevens for too long," Murdock said pensively. "We're due to hit box-cars this coming winter or next. There's too many cattle out here. I plan to ship a lot this fall. Suggest you do the same, Bucky."

"A bad winter?" The rancher shrugged. "Prices are down. Anyway, I don't run as many cattle as you do, Jake. Though a bad winter will wipe a lot of us out."

"Well pencil-pusher, let's hit the sack. We've got a

long ride ahead of us tomorrow. Bucky, you coming along?"

"I'll do that. Need a change of cooking anyway."

"What you need is something besides that bowl haircut."

Chapter Seven

Crowheart and ranchers O'Connor and Murdock reined up abreast one another under a noonday sun on a draw opening onto Medora. They hadn't pushed their horses as cowhands would have done to get there. Murdock's comment that a few new buildings were going up was snatched away by a wind pushing at their backs.

The cow town lay on a flat plain girded by the Little Missouri River, tracks of the Northern Pacific railroad, the stagecoach road and the few lanes running out to the ranches. There was little shrubbery, natural growing or planted by those residing there, just the errant trees cropping up here and there amongst the buildings. On one side of town lay a church, opposite the depot hemmed in by a train on the main line and boxcars taking a breather on a siding. The main buildings were long, two-storied affairs, tended by sheds and outhouses, and not standing along the traditional main street but spread out independently. In the background towered the brick chimney marking the Marquis de Mores meat packing plant; isolated on an elevation stood the Chateau de Mores.

To the west and near the river was located an army

camp abandoned by the U.S. Army and called the Cantonment, marked by wooden barracks and the sutler's store. Another settlement, Little Missouri, a hangout for outlaws, was also there, as was the Pyramid Hotel.

"We're both misplaced Texans, Bucky. Wish you hadn't left?"

"Home is where Martha wants to be." He followed Jake Murdock's eyes staring beyond the sunken recesses of Medora at the westward rolling buttes. One could discern clearly the bold colors in the nearer buttes: blue, yellow, white, and black. Farther out these tints merged into a mellow lavender, and far away to the southwest where the moon stood like a daystar over the Badlands, the hills rippled into a vague and mysterious paleness. Now the wind swept them off the bluff and along a trail beaten by hoof and wagon.

"Crowheart, I'll expect we'll be lodging at the Rough Riders Hotel. The town'll be packed, so it just might be you'll have to stay elsewhere."

"I've bunked out in stables and worse, Mr. Murdock."

"You ain't no orphan at that type of life."

They found a stable and some other ranchers just dismounting in front of it, and friendly greetings and some jokes were exchanged as the men went about stabling their horses. What struck Crowheart right off about Medora was the sense of peacefulness it threw off, something that made a man slow down his pace and bask in the barest of breezes while getting the lay of the place. Another piece of that lonely feeling he'd been carting along shredded away. A change of clothing for the ranchers had been packed in their saddlebags, and they brought these with them over to the Rough Riders Hotel. As Murdock had anticipated, most of the rooms had been taken; but he managed to secure one for himself and Bucky O'Connor, and he brought Crowheart aside in the lobby and handed the waddy some money.

"There are a couple of boarding houses," said the rancher. "And just west of here the Pyramid Hotel. But I'd shy away from that place and Little Misery, as it's a known hangout for buffalo hunters and others wanting to part a man from his money. Won't be much taking place this afternoon. Tonight, however, the Marquis is throwing a feed for us over at his chalet. You'll be there, Crowheart, and somewhat sober, I might add." Winking, the rancher went after O'Connor, heading for a staircase.

As Crowheart opened the door to leave, he almost bumped into a spectacled rancher crossing the boardwalk. A square-jawed man with a trim mustache and a steady gaze in his eyes, the rancher said as he stepped aside, "Expect you've got the right-of-way here."

Johnny Crowheart had heard the Hashknife tell about and describe the owner of the ranch located just west of them, the Elkhorn Ranch, that the man was a New Yorker come out here to regain his health. From what Crowheart could see now, Teddy Roosevelt looked robust and tanned by the sun, and Crowheart stammered, "Sorry to get in your way, Mr. Roosevelt."

"I don't believe we've met before?"

"Names Crowheart—work for Jake Murdock."

"My pleasure," Roosevelt said loudly but in a

friendly way. "Glad that Jake could make it. But then again, he's been very supportive of the association. See you around, Crowheart."

The fact that a man of Roosevelt's stature would take time to exchange small talk with him brought an appreciative smile from Crowheart as he sauntered down the street. One veteran puncher, as relayed to Crowheart by Ike Walton, had spoken of Roosevelt thusly, that the four-eyed maverick has sand in his craw a-plenty. And since Ike Walton had also spoken highly of the Oyster Grotto, and that segundo Bill Lowman had been mooning over a certain waitress working there, Crowheart decided to check both the food and the woman out.

Along the way, he sauntered past the saloon, the Plainsman, where he'd had that disagreement with buffalo hunter Yakima Pierce. He couldn't help thinking of Carrie Morgan, also. Downstreet, two men were just unhitching four horses from the Medora-Deadwood stagecoach, and rolling past Crowheart went a democratic wagon, a two seater with a place in the back to hold supplies. From the south came a four-wheeled carriage known as a Dearborn, trailing dust and being pulled at a canter by a pair of matched greys. A lot of horses were idling at hitching racks strung along the street. From nearby came the quick tattoo of a snare drum, and then a tuba began farting a tune onto the street. Tomorrow, according to Murdock, there was to be a parade as part of the festivities to be put on by the Badlands Stockman's Association and to welcome the coming of a new spring.

As it was still the dinner hour, upon entering the

Oyster Grotto restaurant Johnny was forced to wait with another couple on a wooden bench. Most of the diners appeared to be in the cattle trade, though scattered throughout the large dining room were suited men and some in rougher garb, perhaps men hired on at the meat packing plant. Four waitresses scurried back and forth from the kitchen — presiding over the cash register was Blood-Red John Warns. After easing down at a table just vacated by a trio of merchants, Crowheart checked the menu over, and when a waitress appeared, he ordered a t-bone with all the trimmings and chicory coffee.

To his surprise, a different waitress brought his order to the table, and he returned her inquisitive smile as she inquired, "Weren't you one of those hiring on at the Hashknife?"

Crowheart knew right away this had to be the waitress the segundo was sparking, and he said, "Still out there. Tell me, are you . . . Jo Ann?"

"Why, yes," She was an attractive woman with honey-blond hair pinned to her shapely head, the white blouse closed at the neck by a brooch, and a belt gripping her slender waist, the skirt trailing to the floor. She didn't have on makeup, and Johnny reckoned that she didn't need any.

"Mr. Lowman sends his greetings," he lied.

She laughed lightly, and said, "Did he now?"

"Well, not really," he blushed. "He . . . Bill was too busy to come along."

"Mr. Lowman is very sober-minded," she agreed. "And you are?"

"Oh, sorry. Johnny . . . Crowheart."

"Nice meeting you, Johnny. I have some orders to

get out. Have a nice time here."

He watched her hurrying back to the kitchen, and then he bent to the task at hand. The meal, as he'd expected, was delicious, and after leaving a tip for the waitress and going over and paying Blood-Red John, who gave him a cold, appraising look, Crowheart found the street, and farther along, Genial Jim's Billiard Bar.

The clicking of cue balls carried Johnny past the bar and the few poker tables. There were four billiard tables, three being used, with Johnny racking the balls on the idle one. It wasn't too long ago that he'd been a half-hearted pool hustler, picking up a buck here and there in his wanderings through the West. But to his chagrin he found that pool and booze didn't blend, that those challenging him to eight ball or straight pool did so while under the influence. When they invariably lost to Crowheart, there came temper tantrums followed by fisticuffs or naked steel or guns. And venturing alone into a cow town, the angry loser had his own bunch coming right behind to help him stomp the lights out of Crowheart. Anymore, he rarely picked up a cue stick. But the warning from the bossman about him staying relatively sober had carried Johnny into Genial Jim's.

Sawing at reins and roping had stiffened Crowheart's hands and muscled up his arms. It took him several racks to get the feel of the cue and his stroke back. A barmaid had been keeping him supplied with steins of beer, but he drank sparingly. As he turned from the table to take the rack off a wall peg, a cowhand sauntered over and smiled at Crowheart.

"You've shot before."

"Haven't we all," Johnny said vaguely, not really wanting to play pool with the man. "You here for the stockman's meeting, too?"

"Same's you, I reckon. I'm Backus from the 777."

"Crowheart . . . workin' at the Hashknife."

"A quarter a game won't hurt nobody too much—"

"Just so it stays at that."

"Call it—"

"Tails."

"Guess I break."

Crowheart's break scattered the balls, the seven ball scooting into a side pocket. Smoothly he brought his cue tracking after the remaining low balls, then he banked the eight ball into a corner pocket and caught the quarter flipped at him by waddy Backus. "You racked them awful tight for me to get a break like that."

"Well, Johnny, you're better than I thought." As he spoke, others who'd been playing or watching drifted over and settled into chairs along the wall or stood there. "You didn't try to hustle me. Shucks, let's go at it again."

Johnny won five more games running before he was challenged by another waddy, an older man, maybe in his late thirties, and ramrod lean. This time the game was a lot closer, but it was Crowheart sinking the eight ball again. The man who'd lost, T.O. Addison, and as Johnny found out later, the foreman out at the OX spread, placed his cue gently on the green felt cloth and threw Crowheart a congenial smile while extending his hand.

"Nice shooting."

"Thanks."

"There aren't any here in Genial Jim's in your class. Backus, what say you and I drag Johnny here over to that table and discuss a little business proposition."

"Such as taking on that Little Misery pool shark?"

"I believe that is what I had in mind, Mr. Backus."

"Look, fellas, I don't know about this. . . ." Reluctantly, Johnny sat down with the other waddies at a card table, and after a round of drinks had been consumed, he was still firm in his mind not to get involved in a pool match. He watched as those seated and gathered around the table, by request of ranch foreman Addison, dropped what money they had on the table.

"Crowheart, amongst us we've got a little over two hundred dollars."

"That's a heap of money to loose."

"We ain't gonna loose," Backus said firmly.

"Who's the competition?"

"Big Mike Delavan. He's good" — T.O. Addison shoved his round-brimmed hat back and settled lower in the chair — "darned good, I'd say. Beaten all of us here once or twice; cleaned out ol' Ripley, there, just last week. Just don't want to disillusion you as to Big Mike's shootin' abilities."

Despite himself, and his resistance to getting involved in this, a grin spread across Johnny's face. "You sound, T.O., like a politician pulling out all the stops. So you'll back me?"

"Plus you'll get ten percent of our winnings."

"Well, Johnny?"

"Oh," he frowned and rubbed the back of his neck, "I guess so."

As smiles broke out around the table, waddy

Backus reached over and whisked Crowheart's glass of beer away. "We want you clear-eyed for that match. Any cue here you want to bring along?"

"Cue?" Shoving his chair away from the table, T.O. Addison, a cigarette dangling from his lips, went up to the bar and began conferring with the man tending it. After a few minutes he came back toting a black case some two feet in length which he placed carefully on the table. "Gents, feast your eyes upon the weapon Crowheart's gonna use to wipe out Big Mike's little nest egg." He open the case.

Reposing in red velvet was a jointed cue stick, halved by metal inserts, adorned with fancy scrollwork and lacquered to a gleaming finish. The comment of waddy Backus spoke for all of them.

"That is truly a work of art!"

"I know some cowpokes would sell their best saddle for something like that."

"Meaning you, Backus," a waddy said flatly as the others laughed.

"Could be." then Backus joined in while reaching out and picking up the separate parts of the cue stick and screwing them together. "Yup, it truly could be."

"Roscoe, Genial Jim said we could use his wagon to get over to Little Misery. Why don't you and Benny go out back and throw a harness on that horse. Johnny, suggest you practice some with that cue stick a-fore we go calling on Big Mike Delavan. And you others, gather around close, as we have to plan a little strategy."

"Shucks, T.O., why don't we just head over and get to it?"

"Because, Mr. Ripley, Big Mike has a lot of his

blacklegs hanging around just in case things don't go right for him. Now, how's this for openers, gents?"

The high-sided delivery wagon borrowed from Genial Jim carried the waddies away from Medora and westward on a rutted land. They were in a boisterous mood, and it was with some effort that T.O. Addison quieted them down.

"You don't have to act like danged fools all the time," he told them. "Especially you, Roscoe, with them infernal bird calls. Simmer down now, the lot of you. You know the plan."

"That we're to drop off from time to time and sneak into Little Misery by our lonesomes."

"Gee, Roscoe, that was good. So's you and Benny can drop off first. And remember, just don't beeline over to Big Mike's place. Pay your respects at some other saloons first. Well git, Roscoe!"

The cowhands jumped from the moving wagon and found some underbrush and another route into Little Missouri spread haphazardly along the river. As the wagon rolled along, other waddies spilled out and darted away. It was still light out, the sun at least a couple of hours from setting and, Crowheart figured, enough time for him to play this pool match, then return to Medora and accompany the ranchers over to the Chateau de Mores.

Fording the river, the wagon rumbled into Little Missouri, with Crowheart crouched alone in the back and on the front seat, Ripley holding the reins and T.O. Addison touching flame to another cigarette. Over by the Northern Pacific tracks and just past the depot stood the Pyramid Park Hotel. Tethered before the hotel were several horses and one harnessed to a carriage. Johnny was a good judge of horseflesh, knew he'd seen that big bay standing there before, and probably over at Medora. Some of the brands on the other horses were unknown to him, but most of those horses looked thinned out and trailworn. This was a known hangout for longriders, drifters and bunco artists. So the men riding those horses had either just arrived or had plans to leave in a hurry. He looked at the bay again, then it struck him that the horse could belong to Yakima Pierce. He wasn't looking forward to another encounter with the buffalo hunter.

Farther along amid the few mercantile stores were an abundance of saloons, the Elk, and Western House, among others. Ripley swung the wagon around and brought it on the shaded side of the Western House. Everyone swung down from the wagon. After tying the reins to a post, Ripley stepped to where Addison was chatting with Crowheart.

Patting a hand against the black case containing the cue stick, Addison said, "That's Delavan's place yonder, The Senate. I'll head over there and set things up. Give me about a half hour."

"Sure this'll work?"

"To Big Mike you'll be just another drunken cowpoke looking for some action at his tables."

"Sure," said Ripley, "just slop a little whiskey on your shirt, Johnny, and the smell alone will convince that pool shark."

"Okay," said Crowheart, "but it's been a spell since I've shot pool for more'n a glass of beer and change." Rippling through him was this sense of apprehension that Big Mike would beat him, and bad. "I'm a little rusty."

"Rusty or not, Johnny, you're aces and eights better'n any of us." Leaving them alongside the Western House, Addison headed downstreet.

Crowheart, glancing again at those horses idling before the Pyramid Park Hotel, had this sudden impulse to head over for a closer look; but Ripley sauntering toward a saloon across the street made him drop the idea, and he hurried to catch up with the other waddy.

They entered the saloon, one cramped room holding only three tables, a bar and a slot machine being played by a hardcase. After ordering whiskey for himself and Crowheart, Ripley managed to spill his glass on the front of Johnny's shirt, and he mumbled an apology while signalling the barkeep to refill his glass. Seated at one of the tables was a thin man riffling a deck of worn cards and clad in a threadworn suit. Around the cigarillo he shaped a sneer and said, "Guess some fools can't hold their whiskey."

The waddy shifted around and asked in innocent tones, "You talking to me?"

"Your mama give you that gun?"

"You mean this hunk of iron thonged down here?" Ripley downed his whiskey. "All I use it for, sir, is to pound nails and crack walnuts and rap smart-mouths like you alongside the head."

As the gambler brushed the tail of his black coat aside, Crowheart eased out his sixgun and took one step over to the hardcase who'd been dropping nickels in the slot machine, the barrell of Crowheart's weapon ramming into the man's back. "Mister," he said, turning to the gambler, "either leather that gun you're holding or I'll drop your pardner where he stands."

"It seems," Ripley said to the gambler, "you just got your insurance policy cancelled. Wanna renew it?"

Carefully the man seated at the card table placed both of his hands flat on the table so that the waddy could see them, and then he flinched when Ripley's swiftly drawn gun barked and punched out the center of the ace of spades.

"Bardog," Ripley said kindly as if nothing had happened, "A round of drinks, my friend, the gambler, is treating. Sure nice to come into a town and have the welcome wagon waiting and all. Yup, surely nice." He downed his drink, as did Crowheart, then both waddies backed out the door and sought another saloon.

"Thanks for holding off that other one."

"My pleasure," said Crowheart.

"How'd you know they was working together?"

"The barkeep had restless eyes."

Approaching a saloon called the Elk, Crowheart chanced to glance in a front window, with his warning hand stopping his companion. Softly he asked "See those men seated at that back table?"

"Where that dude is wearing a derby?"

"The next table."

"Yeah, them's the Morgans; wolfers, I hear, or sodbusters. Both have a certain stench to it."

"They sure want my scalp. There more to your name than Ripley?"

"Oh, sure, got four other names clotheslining before Ripley—but shortened all of that to Mort. The word's out them Morgans are holding hands with some outlaws. See that fancy-dressed dude sitting with them?"

"Looks awful young."

"That be the son of your bossman."

"Darin Murdock?"

"Yup. Heard the kid was away at some college."

There were two other men clustered around the table, and judging from the way they sat and looked, outlaws. One of them was sort of handsome and wearing a cattleman's leather coat; he seemed to be doing most of the talking. Briefly, he studied the son of Jack Murdock, and saw that Darin had his father's deepset eyes, which at the moment were flushed with drink. He could almost sense Yakima Pierce's presence here in Little Missouri, too, and the thought troubled Johnny. It could be that Darin Murdock had just stumbled into this bar, and seeing an easy mark, those he was seated with were letting him treat them to drinks. But, somehow, Crowheart felt there was a deeper reason.

"Well, Johnny, we'd best make tracks for Big Mike's."

"Sure," he said uneasily, his mind more on young Murdock that the coming pool match.

Farther along the street, T.O. Addison was being scrutinized by others strung along the long bar in The Senate Billiard Parlor. Tending bar were a couple of barkeeps while glowering over at Addison was Big Mike's bouncer, a rawboned lineman fired by the Northern Pacific for stealing. The place wasn't as fancy as Genial Jim's, but larger and darker and reeking with hostility. Most of the games going on in The Senate were crooked, and if anyone complained or accused the dealers of cheating, either the bouncer or other toughs hired by Big Mike would settle the matter in an unkindly fashion. This had happened to some of Addison's men, and other cowpokes. A few had simply disappeared. The only law was that of the gun, and these hardcases reveled in that. Someone had once remarked that the going price for murder was ten bucks, though from glancing around at those crowing the place, T.O. Addision felt that was a trifle steep. Because he was known here, and had the reputation of not backing down from anyone, nobody came up to hustle Addison. He also knew that by now word of his presence had been carried to Big Mike Delavan.

When a barkeep finally came over, Addison drawled, "I see you've got in some Carstair's Best."

"Just last week."

"Bring a bottle of that and a glass of beer back to that billiard table." He opened the case to show the cue and smiled up at the barkeep. "Just arrived from Chicago. Tell Big Mike I'm here."

"I expect he already knows that. And I don't deliver drinks to the pool players."

"You'll deliver mine," Addison said coldly. "Put it on my tab." He smiled his way back to the billiard tables as it was the custom at The Senate not to give credit, the slogan being CASH AND CARRY. On a nearby table he set the case and removed the cue, placing it on one of the billiard tables as he proceeded to rack the balls. Drifting out of the shadows, came a trio of toughs, the men stationing themselves to sort of hem in the waddy but staying clear of the billiard table. This told him that Big Mike was on the way.

Some of the waddies betting on Johnny Crowheart also put in an appearance, stepping to the bar or spreading around and watching the action at the gaming tables. Chalking the cue, Addison tipped his hat back some and bent to the table. He broke the balls, then began shooting slowly, tipping the angry barkeep when the man brought over the drinks he had ordered.

"I tell you, Mort, I can beat anybody in this dump!"

T.O. Addison turned from the table and some of the customers looked at the front entrance as waddies Ripley and Crowheart staggered through the batwings to plant their boots on sawdust. A scowl ripped across Addison's forehead when those who'd just entered headed toward him and the billiard tables.

"Mort Ripley, you ought to be ashamed of yourself getting liquored up like that," complained Addison.

"Hey, it warn't my idea. Just ran into my old drinkin' pard, Crowheart here. Crowheart hears them balls clicking, he's just gotta get himself a game of . . . of pool." Laughing, he clapped Johnny on the back. "Well, here you is, pard."

Reeling forward, Crowheart poked a finger into Addison's chest and muttered disdainfully, "You, I don't like your nose."

"There's no call for talk like that, sport," he said calmly. "Could you breathe on somebody else."

"Say," chortled Crowheart, "lookee here." He stared down at the fancy cue Addison was holding. "Fancy, fancy . . . hey, Mort, that cue's longer than this gent's nose."

"Sport, in your condition you wouldn't recognize

98

your own horse . . . or which direction it's pointing."
He shoved away from Crowheart and picked up the
chalk.

"Then maybe you'll recognize this," said Johnny as
he pulled a thick wad of money out of his shirt
pocket. "I'm here for some action, fancy cue. Or
maybe you're all wind."

"Seems uncommonly strange for a drifter like you
to have so much money. Ripley, your friend a bank
robber or something?" Addison laughed coldly at
Crowheart, then he added, "Alright, how's about
eight ball . . . say, fifty bucks a game?"

"One game of nine ball for the whole bundle,"
Johnny said recklessly.

"Reckon, sport, I don't have that much. Mort,
could you lend me some. 'Cause playing this drunk'll
be like money in the bank."

"Doggone, T.O., I'm tapped out."

"Seems that leaves just me to play this big spender."
The crowd which had gathered around the billiard
tables parted to allow a tall, gaunt man chomping on
a cigar through. Big Mike Delavan was clean-shaven.
Acne blotches pitted his lower face as did a couple of
scars ridging across his nose and forehead, which told
Crowheart the man was used to violence. Unlike most
of the men in the place, he was immaculate in white
linen and black broadcloth. He wore no rings on long
tapering fingers reaching for a house cue.

"It seems, T.O., your friend is itching for some
action."

Addison snorted, "He's no friend of mine. If you
want to scalp him, Big Mike, have a go at it. Why, I'll
even let this sport use my cue."

"I don't know, Johnny," cautioned Mort Ripley, "about playing Delavan. Why don't we head back to Medora—"

"No way," said Crowheart as the cue Addison had borrowed from Genial Jim was passed to him. Johnny fumbled for a piece of chalk and knocked it to the floor. He bent to retrieve it and chalked the cue while grinning at Delavan across the table. "Being this is your table and I ain't never shot on it a-fore, how's about giving me some odds?"

"Why should I," Big Mike said through a cold smile.

"I don't know, Big Mike," broke in Addison. I saw this waddy knock some balls around over at Genial Jim's; he's awful good. When he's sober." He'd added that last bit just to sink the hook a little deeper into Big Mike Delavan. He knew that if Crowheart had wandered in here alone, the waddy would have left broke and probably horizontal. Hooking two fingers around the shot glass perched by the bottle of Carstair's Best, he drank it straight as Delavan dipped a hand under his lapel and pulled out a wallet thick with greenbacks.

"You wanted to shoot nine ball—"

"Yup, one game, winner take all." Bending over the pool table, Crowheart stroked the cue a few times and chuckled, then he added, "Unless you've got something else to do?"

"You're awful mouthy," Big Mike said darkly. "But I'll give you two to one odds."

"That all?" Crowheart's response to the offer made by Delavan brought from T.O. Addison a silent groan. "A man with your reputation can do better that that."

Stung by the cowpoke's retort, Big Mike forced a smile. "Alright, three to one—but I get the break."

"Generally we flip to see who breaks. But, alright, we'll play. How about your friend here holding the money? Mort, ain't you gonna back me?"

"I only got fifty bucks, Johnny. Besides, Big Mike shoots a mean stick."

"Don't worry, pardner, I've got this hombre's number."

With a worried shrugging of his shoulders, Mort Ripley took out of a Levi pocket what money he had and handed it to Addison, as did Crowheart, with Big Mike Delavan handing over the money he'd wagered. Then a smug smile showing, Delevan said, "T.O., since you've been elected to hold the money, why don't you rack the balls."

All of the gambling action had ground to a halt as those patronizing The Senate Billiard Parlor drifted over to watch the pool match. While Big Mike and Crowheart had been wrangling over the pool game, Addison had looked to see if the other waddies in on this were in position. They were, but still it was a worried T.O. Addison hunting up the balls in the pockets and placing them in the rack. If Johnny lost, they would just go back to Medora and pour salt on their wounds. Carefully he racked the balls, and stepping away, said, "Your break, Mr. Delavan."

"Cowboy," Big Mike said to Crowheart, "I feel so good about this I'm buying drinks around." Then, his left hand forming a bridge for the cue and arm extended on the billiard table, Delavan ripped the balls apart. He smiled cockily around cigar smoke at the three and five balls spilling into different pockets. Chalking, he surveyed the layout of the remaining balls. The object of the game was to pocket all of the balls in rotation, with the man pocketing the nine ball picking up the money wagered. Swiftly, almost contemptuously, the man set the balls seeking leather pockets until only three remained, the seven, eight and nine. His last shot hadn't given him good position on the seven ball hidden behind the nine ball and wedged against the railing. He could go for the seven, but that might open up the table to his opponent, who was leaning on his cue, gazing at the pool table through half-lidded eyes and swaying a little. Deciding to play a safety, Big Mike sent the white ivory cue ball rolling softly toward the seven ball but missing it deliberately. Now the cue ball came away from the railing to stop at the other end of the table leaving Johnny Crowheart an impossible shot.

He'd expected something of this sort, but allowed a carefree grin to show as he studyied the layout of the balls still on the table. The nine ball lay just up from the seven, and the only shot, a desperate one at that, was banking the seven into the nine to send the nine into the corner pocket up where he stood. "What do you think, Mort?"

Ripley, standing just behind him, muttered, "All you can do is play a safety like Big Mike just done. Just don't get reckless, Johnny."

"Reckless is my middle name, pardner." Through the harsh glaring lamplight splashing down upon the green felt cloth, Crowheart bent over his cue stick, with his eyes seeking Big Mike's. "Combination, pool shark — the seven into the nine" — he patted the corner pocket—"and into this big old basket."

"Tough shot, cowboy," spat out Delavan. There was the briefest inkling of worry, which passed as Crowheart reeled against the table while studying the shot again.

There was concern in Johnny's mind, too, that if by some miracle he made the shot, all Hades was certain to break loose in here. His eyes tracking down the vast expanse of green cloth, he leaned into the shot again, screening out the bystanders and Big Mike's leering face. At that moment it suddenly dawned on Crowheart that he would make the shot, and for the biggest stakes he'd ever played for. Sighting down the cue, he stroked it to send the cue ball spinning into the seven. Darting away from the railing, the seven struck the nine, and it headed straight for the corner pocket and nestled into it.

"Doggonit!" yelled Mort Ripley. "You done it, pardner!"

On the opposite side of the table, the face of Big Mike Delavan spoke of his disbelief and sudden rage.

"Now you've got to deal with me, Crowheart!"

It wasn't Delavan who'd spoken, but Joe Bob Morgan shoving some onlookers aside and bringing the sixgun to bear on Crowheart. Behind Joe Bob came his brothers, Trace and Abe, who were as flushed with drink as he was. The young sodbuster said, "Crowheart, me and my brothers are gonna geld you for doing harm to our sister!" As his brothers fanned out, Joe Bob holstered his handgun and produced a Barlow knife, then he pulled the long blade out of the elk-bone handle and laughed menacingly.

A quiet nudge from T.O. Addison brought Ripley

103

easing back into the crowd, and screened by others, Addison unleathered his Colt .45 and whispered, "unleather yours, Mort, and get ready."

"Didn't expect nothing like this."

"Neither did Big Mike."

"Just hope that wagon's out back."

"Just hope Crowheart can handle that drunken sodbuster."

Backing away from the pool table, Crowheart bumped into a chair and lost his balance. The sodbuster came in fast, his knife swiping at Johnny but missing. He followed this with a loping right to Crowheart's head that threw him back against the wall, and again he managed to elude the knife, spinning away, suddenly remembering the cue he was clutching. When he spun back the butt of the cue was coming at Joe Bob's head. It struck solidly drawing blood and shattering; the sodbuster plummeted to the floor and lay still.

But Addison's gun hand didn't, as he swung the barrel of his Colt .45 ceilingward and pulled the trigger. The heavy report of his weapon froze everyone, and Addison called out to Abe and Trace Morgan, "Drop 'em, boys. Or I'll gut-shoot the pair of you. That's it . . . no sense getting killed over this. Come on, Crowheart, hustle back here."

"Addison, I want my money."

He yelled back at Big Mike Delavan, "Just come over to Medora and try gettin' it."

The other waddies had disarmed Big Mike's toughs, and they began backing down a back passageway, with Addison spilling out last, the closing door striking at his boot heels. Piling into the waiting wagon, he said, "Alright, Roscoe, lay whip to them horses."

They kept watching their backtrail until the river had been crossed, and then Mort Ripley let out a relieved whistle and yelled, "That was some hoedown."

"Did you see the look on Big Mike's face when he realized he'd been hustled. Never thought I'd see the day. And that shot Crowheart made . . . that was something."

"Made my day," said Addison. Then he turned to Crowheart, "I'm real sorrowful that you had to mangle Genial Jim's cue."

"I was real desperate at the time."

"That eye's starting to close. Good thing it happened after that pool match. Just why were those Morgans after your hide, Johnny?"

"Hey, we're coming into town."

Ripley's call swung everyone's eyes to onlookers gazing curiously at a bunch of cowhands crowding Genial Jim's freight wagon, and it also kept Johnny Crowheart from responding to Addison's question. Knowing the caliber of men the Morgans were, he could understand their not believing what Carrie had told them as to why she hadn't come home until morning, and they were the same caliber that would rather ambush a man at night than in broad daylight or in a crowded barroom. From what he'd seen in Little Missouri, it was no longer any rumor that the Morgans were hanging out with outlaws.

What troubled Crowheart more than the Morgan brothers going after him was Darin Murdock being over there. Being he was young and foot-loose, it just could be that Jake Murdock's son was out for a good time before returning to the ranch. Though he wasn't about to pass judgement on Darin Murdock, Crowheart had the uneasy feeling it was more than Darin passing a Friday afternoon with the Morgan brothers. The more he chewed on it, the more he felt that young Murdock was involved in shady business. Maybe that feeling came from the fact Darin Murdock had been engaged in lawless activities back east.

When he'd viewed the Morgan brothers sitting with Darin Murdock in that saloon, he could have been watched himself, which would explain why the Morgan brothers had turned up at The Senate Billiard Parlor, and would mean his hunch had been right about Yakima Pierce being in Little Missouri. These men were setting up some crooked game, and snared in it was Darin Murdock, and with him, Johnny Crowheart, now a marked man.

Chapter Eight

"I don't expect you ran into a door, Crowheart."

"It wasn't that a-tall, Mr. Murdock," he said sheepishly. Johnny's left eye had puffed closed, and he'd tugged the brim of his hat low over his forehead. The ranchers had just emerged from the Rough Riders Hotel into dusk painting the buttes and cloudy sky.

"Would you care to tell us about it?"

He fell into step with Murdock. "Actually, it started over at Genial Jim's—where I let some waddies talk me into a pool match. Addison and—"

"That, I expect, will be T.O. Addison. Reliable enough, but prone to raise heck at times."

"Actually the match didn't take place at Genial Jim's."

"Actually, Crowheart, where did this take place?"

"Jake," said Bucky O'Connor, "this is gettin' real interesting."

"Shaping up that way. Don't tell me Addison dragged you over to Little Misery—"

"That's about it, Mr. Murdock," Crowheart had to admit. "Took on Big Mike Delavan."

"Son, you ought to have more sense that that. Maybe I should'a left you back at the ranch bogging out cattle. I expect you lost what I gave you, and everything else you had."

"We pooled our money together . . . around three hundred and—"

"Oh, Lordy, too bad you ain't a cattle buyer. I'd make a killing selling beef to you."

"Played him one game of nine ball—and came up winners."

The rancher stopped in mid-stride, as did Bucky O'Connor, and then Murdock grasped Johnny's arm and stared him right in the eye, for in Jake Murdock's was pure disbelief. "Let me get this straight, Crowheart. You went over to Little Misery, against my express wishes, I might add, and took on Big Mike Delavan in his own place. Is that about it?"

"Yessir, that actually is what happened."

"Bucky, can you believe this?"

"It does leave a person wondering. So then Big Mike gave you that shiner?"

"Joe Bob Morgan done that," Johnny said, following the ranchers into the livery stable and veering over to his horse.

"Seems you had a busy afternoon," said Murdock. "How does Joe Bob Morgan enter into this?"

Johnny had decided not to tell the rancher about seeing his son, Darin, over in Little Missouri. He had a hunch that Darin Murdock knew his father was in Medora. From what ranch foreman Bill Lowman had told him about Murdock's son, Darin hated ranching and his father, and perhaps Jake Murdock had shipped the boy off to college in an attempt to settle him down. Only the opposite had happened.

"Morgan thinks I wronged his sister."

"Did you?" Murdock asked curtly.

"Nossir," he said right back. "But I learned a long time ago you don't reason with a redneck."

This brought quiet laughter from O'Connor. "Wisdom comes with old age, alright."

"I suppose, son, you didn't take time to get a room?" Murdock finished tightening the cinch on his saddle and dropped the stirrup down.

"Haven't gotten around to that."

"Crowded as the town is, you'll wind up sleeping in this stable after all. So much for youthful wisdom." Leading his horse out of the stable, Murdock climbed into the saddle. "Lordy, Crowheart, here we are, heading up to the Marquis' chalet for a high society supper, and you've got that shiner, and probably haven't taken the time to wash up either."

"Done that," he said lamely. "Suppose I could just stay here and eat over at the Oyster Grotto."

"No," the rancher said wearily, "you'll just manage to find some other trouble to get involved in. Still can't believe you bested Big Mike."

The Chateau de Mores seemed as aloof as its owner, something Crowheart was to find out that evening, with the chateau rising elegantly above the river on a flat shelf of grassy plateau. Backgrounding the chateau were layers of buttes blued by twilight. One star had appeared, dimly hugging the southern horizon. Clattering toward the rambling building, servants were there to take their horses.

Awkwardly Johnny followed the ranchers, ambling toward a covered porch running around the main part of the chateau. One wing curled away from the two-storied building with its shuttered windows and red roof touched by dimming sunlight. He felt more out of place when he stepped onto the covered porch to discover, except for some ranch foremen, he was the only lowly waddy there. A servant came over to take their hats, with Crowheart fumbling his into the man's hand, and then over stepped Antoine de Vallombrosa. The Marquis was a dark, handsome Frenchman with a military bearing. Vallombrosa had eagle eyes and waxed mustaches, a silken shirt under a fringed buckskin coat coming over tan trousers tugged into black riding boots.

"Evening, de Mores," said Jake Murdock.

"A pleasure having you here, gentlemen," he said cordially.

"This place looks better everytime I see it. A fellow rancher, Bucky O'Connor. The waddy with the shiner is Crowheart."

Haughtily the Marquis said, "Yes, ranching can be a dangerous business. Especially with the Badlands overrun with outlaws. I'm disappointed you gentlemen didn't respond to my letter of last month."

"Got your letter alright," said O'Connor, as the Marquis beckoned a servant over. "But the price you offered me for my cattle is way below what I can get back east."

"I'll make you a better offer," the Frenchman said suavely. "Selling them to my meat packing enterprise saves you time and money. I do hope you gentlemen like champagne; imported from France."

Lifting a glass from the tray held by a servant, Murdock sipped at the champagne, "Tastes kind of flat, de Mores. Your letter also suggested we align ourselves with that Montana bunch in an attempt to stop this rustling."

"Granville Stuart suggested that."

"That Montana rancher is sure throwing a big shadow. I say let Montana take care of its own lawlessness."

"A lot of Montana and Wyoming lawbreakers are hiding out here in the Badlands, Mr. Murdock. I'll bring this up at tomorrow's meeting."

"Won't object to that, de Mores." Jake Murdock nodded as the Marquis excused himself and went to greet others who'd just arrived. Grimacing at the glass he held, the rancher beckoned a servant over. "You got any whiskey on that tray?"

"Nossir. But we have sour mash or brandy."

"Got any corn liquor?"

"I believe so."

"Then sneak some out here."

As the servant went into the chateau, Crowheart sauntered along the porch to where he had a view of Medora, light seeping out of windows, and the place he'd been this afternoon, the outlaw hangout Little Misery. Near the railroad trestle above the river he could still make out wooden crosses marking Graveyard Butte. All of the ranchers' talk about outlaws and rustling had burred him into a worried frame of mind. Seeing Murdock's son drinking with the Morgans and those longriders hadn't helped either. Staring at the man he worked for, Johnny knew that loyalty meant telling Jake Murdock his son had come home. But the Marquis calling them in to supper brought him drifting in with the other cattlemen.

Crowheart reached to slick a lock of hair back when his boots touched upon red carpeting. He settled onto a chair at a table covered with laced linen and on it polished silverware and China embossed with the Vallombrosa seal. Settling down just across from him was the Marquis' wife, Medora, and to her right, the rancher he'd spoken to this afternoon, Teddy Roosevelt.

"Well, Mr. Crowheart, we meet again." Though Roosevelt took in the black eye, he made no comment.

"You honor me by your presence," said the Marquis as he settled onto a chair at the head of the table. "I believe all of you know one another. But I just want to say that I hope this year all of you wind up in the black. Roosevelt, how were things back in New York?"

"One needs a breather from politics. It's even good to see you Texas rawhides again."

This brought some smiles cracking around the table, for once upon a time rawhide was the derisive name northern cattlemen called Texas cowhands. It referred to the Texans' habit of mending whatever broke down or fell apart on the trail, from a bridle to a wagon tongue, by tying it up with strips of rawhide.

"For certain," said the 777 ranch owner Kile Sandby, "those Texas outfits I worked for sure hated to give up on the grub. All we ever had was cornbread, sowbelly, beans and an empty feeling gnawing at our bellys. Why, I can remember the time . . ."

It was when the servants were bringing in a second course, saddles of venison, that a newcomer in the person of Darin Murdock was escorted into the dining room of the chateau. He was dressed exactly as Crowheart had seen him last, in a tweed suit and eastern hat, but clear-eyed now, and looking about for his father.

Bucky O'Connor said, "Well, you made it after all."

"Just got back," he said around an engaging smile.

"You must join us."

"I'd rather not impose."

"Nonsense," the Marquis insisted. "Just how was Chicago?"

"Splendid. But one gets tired of that kind of life. Father, I suppose you'll be wanting me at the meetings—"

"Why, if you want to come, fine."

Gazing at Jake Murdock, Crowheart could see the questions dancing in the man's eyes. He'd been cautioned by the Hashknife segundo not to let on that he knew about Darin Murdock's escapades back east. Once or twice Johnny had had scrapes with the law himself, so he could sympathize with what had happened to the rancher's son. Perhaps that's all it was, a last fling by Darin Murdock before he headed back to the ranch. Perhaps he was reading too much into having seen Darin over in Little Missouri. But as the evening wore on, with the men taking their ease back on the porch again, from time to time Crowheart could feel the hostile eyes of Darin Murdock upon him.

Around eleven o'clock he told Jake Murdock he was heading back to look for a room and he left, riding away from the chateau and letting his horse pick its way down the sloping trail. As he'd more or less expected, all of the hotels were full, and he was forced to bed down in the loft of the livery stable.

Little did Johnny Crowheart realize as he dropped off to sleep wrapped in his sheepskin and surrounded by the musky smell of hay that his not getting a room earlier would save his life.

Chapter Nine

Moonlight streaming through an upper window in the Hotel De Mores revealed Yakima Pierce wiping blood staining his hunting knife on a pillow. The window was open, but at three in the morning Medora lay sleeping, and only the labored breathing of the mountain man broke the dark silence.

The other man in the room wasn't breathing, just strung up on the closet door. Mort Ripley had still been alive but unconscious when the skinning process had begun. Slowly he'd become aware that something was terribly wrong. And by the time awareness came fully to Mort Ripley, Yakima's sharp knife had already sliced Ripley open from Adam's apple to lower belly and laid back bare skin. With awareness had come the agonizing pain, with his screams cut off by the bandanna gouging into his mouth and tied at the back of his head. Leaving the torso nothing more than raw and bleeding flesh, Yakima had started on the face with his knife, all the time muttering in the Sioux tongue to the man he was torturing. The buffalo hunter was on the verge of slicing out the remaining eye when the waddy made a gurgling noise and died. Cursing, Yakima had turned to the bed and picked up the pillow.

Crouching out through the window onto the sloping roof of the back shed, the buffalo hunter went down the roof and dropped to the ground. Waiting for him was one of the Morgan brothers, who inquired anxiously, "You was gone a long time."

"One's dead," he said indifferently.

"Crowheart?"

"The other one." Yakima swung into the saddle.

"Joe Bob'll be pleased to hear that. Just where do you suppose Crowheart is bunking out?"

"We'll get him. Let's ride."

Another couple of hours passed before there appeared in the lobby of the Hotel De Mores the man sharing room 224 with Mort Ripley. A long poker session had kept T.O. Addison up until now, and he went tiredly up the staircase. He'd been doing alright in the game until an hour ago, then his luck and the cards went sour. But to the foreman of the 777 Spread it had been an enjoyable night, for he was still savoring Johnny Crowheart's outhustling Big Mike Delavan in that game of nine ball.

Upon trying the door, he found it was locked and that he didn't have a key. He rapped a couple of times below the metallic room numbers, and then he said quietly, "Ripley's an awful light sleeper." Now, somewhat nettled, he called out. Maybe, came Addison's thought, his roomie could have picked up a bar girl.

"If this ain't just dandy," Addison scowled as he debated over breaking into the room or going down to the lobby in search of another key. It was shadowy where he stood by the door, and only when he passed alongside a wall lamp did he notice that his left boot was leaving blood markings on the floor. Unhooking the lamp, he carried it back to his room to bring light falling onto a pool of blood that had formed on the door sill. Fearing the worst, he kicked the door open and barged into the room.

"Oh . . . no!"

He was stunned by what he saw hanging from the closet door, where still more blood stained the door and wall and formed bloody trails on the floor. Somehow he managed to get out of the room and stumble down the hallway to the room occupied by the man he worked for, 777 owner Kile Sandby.

He hammered on the door to rattle it while calling out:

"Kile . . . Kile . . . open up! Dammit . . . Kile, open up!"

A key rasped in the lock, then the door was flung open by the rancher, and T.O. Addison stumbled into the room and gasped out, "It's Mort . . . all cut up . . . dead . . . Mort's dead—"

"Get a hold of yourself, T.O. Where's Ripley?"

"Our room." He set the lantern down hard on the dresser and reached for the bottle of whiskey. "Just got done playing poker. Came back here . . . and . . . it's horrible. . . ."

Reaching for the lantern, clad only in his longjohns and holding his sixgun, Kile Sandby hurried out of the door to find Addison's room and the body of one of his cowpunchers. When he came out of room 224, it was to see his foreman coming down the hallway still clutching the bottle of whiskey, and Kile Sandby

117

said in a quaking voice, "That's . . . inhuman. . . ."

"Big Mike? He must have ordered it done?"

"I don't know, Addison, I just don't know. Just can't picture something like this happening over a game of pool."

"I'm going over and brace that—"

The rancher grasped Addison's shoulder and said firmly, "Not tonight. If Big Mike's men did this, they'll be waiting. First we'll take care of Mort. Expect we'll need the undertaker."

"I'll go roust him up."

"I'll get dressed and go with you. And pass me that bottle, T.O., I need some reinforcement."

It wasn't until Johnny Crowheart had left the livery stable, passed through sunlight misting out of a cloudy sky and settled down in a booth at the Cowboy Cafe that he found out about Mort Ripley being murdered. The man who was doing the telling, a merchant seated with others along the counter, told of how Kile Sandby and some of his men, and others, were saddling up right now with the intentions of heading over to Little Missouri. With this still ringing in his ears, Crowheart scrambled out of the booth and beelined back to the livery stable.

He arrived there just as Jake Murdock and rancher O'Connor were saddling their horses, and Murdock said, "I expect you heard?"

"Yup—and that Big Mike done it."

"Maybe. Just maybe."

Murdock's open skepticism set Johnny to having doubts, too, as he saddled Pearly Gate. For some unsettling reason all he could think about was Darin Murdock, the Morgan brothers, and that buffalo hunter, Yakima Pierce. Mort Ripley was dead just because he'd seen Darin Murdock over at the Little Missouri saloon; this had to be the connection. Last night at the Chateau de Mores, the only reason he'd left early was to escape young Murdock's probing eyes. It could be Darin had resented Johnny taking his place. That must be it, and that Darin had no connection to the killing, and all of this would end when they had it out with gambler Delavan.

They found others congregating out in front of Genial Jim's just opening its doors for business, bar and pool. Edging his horse alongside Addison's, Johnny said, "I never expected something like this."

T.O. Addison said vehemently as he checked out the loads in his handgun, "Big Mike'll pay . . . along with those toughs. You should'a seen poor Ripley . . . all cut up like that." A shudder rippled through his body.

"Before we head out," Kile Sandby called out, "I'm gonna tell you men how it's gonna be. We'll call Big Mike out first. Then listen to what he has to say. If we just take Delavan out and hang him . . . well, it's something all of us will have to live with. There's a lot of other scum lurking around here besides Delavan and his bunch."

"He did it all right!"

Sandby glared at a cowhand. "Any more talk like that, mister, and you can stay behind. As of now we're the law out here. So act like it. That's it, gents; mosey along now."

Counting the 777 hands there were over thirty

horsemen cantering past the Rough Riders Hotel and and veering past other buildings to find the road that would take them the short distance to the Little Missouri River and beyond to the man they sought. The sun came warming at their backs. Over in a marshy place came the tink-tink-a-link of a meadow lark, and they could see red-wing blackbirds hopping amongst the reeds. After they'd forded the river, their horses threw up clods of wet mud, and it was around here that Jake Murdock spurred closer to Kile Sandby.

"It's a little early, Kile. Doubt if Big Mike'll be at his place of business. He's got that clapboard house setting north on the fringes of Little Misery. You ever meet his wife?"

"Once upon a time a whore, I've heard."

"Was back a spell. Big Mike sets a lot by her — name's Maybelline. It would be a shame to harm him where she can see it."

"What about his men?"

"They bunk upstairs of the billiard room and some of them in a small house out back. There's about seven or eight of them, not counting the bardogs."

Kile Sandby held up a gloved hand and pulled up to have the others gather around. "Bucky . . ."

"Yeah, Kile?"

"I'll take Jake and Crowheart, and Addison, with me over to Delavan's house. Take the others over to his billiard parlor. But go in easy. Remember, some are staying in that house back of the place. Once we get Big Mike, we'll hustle over there."

Jake Murdock sprinted away from the sun, which appeared in a crack between the scattering clouds. He said heavily, and with a cutting edge to his words,

"Take it cool going in. I don't want any more getting killed. And I don't mean Delavan's men either. Good hands are hard to come by."

With the larger bunch clattering off to the southwest to come in from that direction, Crowheart rode hanging back from Addison, Sandby and Murdock riding abreast of one another past the scattered buildings of Little Missouri. Murdock pointed out Big Mike's house with its tapered roof dusted by sunlight, and when they appeared around a corner it was to find the man they were after slumped on the front porch steps, gazing past them, distantly as someone sunk into deep thought. Then he stirred and gazed blankly at the riders.

"That was a hard price Ripley had to pay, Delavan!" said Kile Sandby.

"Pay? Oh, you mean that pool game? I lost, remember. And to that hustler there, Crowheart, or whatever his name is." He rose with his eyes still containing that puzzled glimmer.

"Cut the crap, Delavan," Addison barked. "You or your men killed Mort Ripley. And we came to hang them and you."

"Who the hell is Mort Ripley?" he retorted angrily.

"Only a man as low as you would kill a man that way."

"When did . . . this happen?"

"Last night," responded Murdock. He was as puzzled as Sandby by the look riding across Big Mike's face. Also, it dawned on Murdock that the man had been up for some time, hence the empty coffee cup and crunched butts of cigarillos filling the cast-iron ashtray perched on a nearby bench.

121

"Sorry, gents, but I was here all night."

"That only proves that your men did the killing!"

Then the attention of the horsemen went to a Medora resident, Doc Henderson, stepping up to stare out through the closed screen door. He came out and said, "Couldn't help overhearing what was being tossed around. Howdy, Murdock, Sandby. I just want to tell Mr. Delavan that his wife seems to be over the worst of it. She's got a bad case of pneumonia."

"He never left here last night?"

"Ever since I got here around ten last night Mr. Delavan never set foot off the premises. Now, if you'll excuse me—"

"That satisfy you," Delavan said bitterly.

"For now," said the owner of the 777 Spread, and he wheeled his horse around and rode away with the others.

"Don't think he was lying."

"Maybe not about leaving the house. But the killing's another matter, Jake. He ain't out of the woods yet."

A few curious eyes followed the ranchers cutting past an outhouse and onto a street where a cowhand waved them behind Big Mike Delavan's billiard emporium. They had all of the toughs and bardogs backed up against a shed wall, with these men standing there in various stages of undress. Kile Sandby told them why Delavan wasn't with them, and about the man's wife being under the weather.

Bucky O'Connor holstered his handgun and said, "None of these men were in Medora last night, or so they say."

"Well, they would have been expecting us to come

over." Sandby scratched along his hairline.

"You ever consider this being a solo effort. Ripley did have some money on him; when drinking he did get careless from time to time."

"You mean someone livin' in Medora or riding through could have killed him?"

"From the looks of this scum," said Jake Murdock, "none of them could carve up a turkey much less do that job on Ripley."

"That narrows it down considerable."

A sort of sinking feeling hit Crowheart in the belly, for somehow he knew just who had killed Mort Ripley. He could still remember that big wicked hunting knife of Yakima Pierce's trying to carve a hunk out of him. But to speak now would involve Jake Murdock's son, and he just might be given his walking papers. What was it that Bill Lowman had told him before, that Darin Murdock hated his father. That hadn't been the case last night at the Chateau de Mores, more of a case of the prodigal son coming home and being welcomed by a pleased but wondering father.

The winds out here in the Badlands were stirring, coming at Johnny Crowheart from all directions, and right now he didn't know which way to turn, or who to go to with what he knew. That it involved Darin Murdock and rustling there was little doubt in Johnny's mind.

The sound of a fist striking bone brought his eyes upon T.O. Addison standing over a fallen tough, and Addison said bitterly, "Alright, scum, talk or I'll hammer your brains into the ground! Who killed Ripley?" As he grabbed a hunk of shirt and hit the man again, some of the waddies closed in and pulled Addison away.

Kile Sandby said softly, "Let it go, Addison. You others, too. The truth'll come out someday. I've made arrangements to have the burial tomorrow morning. I'd appreciate all of you coming to pay final respects to a good man."

Crowheart was somewhat relieved that he didn't have to sit in at the Stockmen's Association meeting presided over by Teddy Roosevelt, which was still going on as Saturday afternoon wound down.

Around eleven that morning the parade highlighted by a brass band with new uniforms furnished by the Marquis de Mores had strutted among the business streets, with a mounted guard of two horsemen out front and displaying the territorial flag and the stars and stripes. Others in wagons, mounted and afoot had straggled behind, along with a mongrel chasing a stray cat through the paraders.

Before the parade there'd been talk of cancelling it, and the fireworks scheduled for tonight, because of Mort Ripley being murdered. Kile Sandby had ended this talk by doffing his hat and remarking as to how Ripley enjoyed a good time same as the next man.

As for townspeople, they'd seen killing before, knew there'd probably be another tomorrow or next week, and hoped that Billings County officials would quit dragging their feet and organize its government. Now any lawbreaker was taken the forty miles to Dickinson.

Crowheart wasn't in the mood for drinking, or

playing pool, and at the moment he was idling away the noon hour at Genial Jim's with some of the cowpokes he'd met, although T.O. Addison wasn't there but over at the meeting. They'd pulled a couple of tables together. All of them were drinking coffee furnished free by the barkeep except for Roscoe Backus, who had a stein of beer.

"I've heard Indians doing that . . . skinning a man."

"Me too, Roscoe."

"Like Jake Murdock said," commented another, "somebody had to have a real hate to do Ripley thataway."

"Some are just naturally mean."

"I still think Big Mike did it."

"It fits his character."

Johnny refilled his cup from the coffee pot and said, "I've been wondering—any of you seen the Morgan brothers around town today? Or that buffalo hunter, Yakima Pierce?"

"It surely would be hard to miss a bunch like that. Nope, Johnny, can't say that I have."

"That Morgan . . . that Joe Bob wanted a hunk of you real bad, Crowheart. Just what did you do to his sister?" Roscoe Adamson smiled at Johnny over the rim of his glass.

"Not a danged thing, Roscoe. She's a fine woman."

"Awful pretty, too."

"I snuck up to that room." Everyone looked at OX Spread cowpoke Hank Bennington. "They still hadn't cleaned the blood away. A man with a real big knife or one of them machetes must have been used on poor Mort."

"I feel kind'a talked out about it," said Johnny as he shoved the chair back and came to his feet. "Obliged for the company."

Johnny and three other cowpokes stepped outside into air freshened by a passing rain shower. The sky was clearing, with a gust of wind fetching up the pleasant scent of spring ripening into summer. A suited man approached Genial Jim's detoured around a puddle and called out to them.

"Addison said I'd probably find you gentlemen over here."

"I don't see any gentlemen. Do you, Johnny?"

"Nope."

"I'm Arthur Packard, the—"

"Yeah, you're ramrodding the Badlands Cowboy. I suppose this is about the killing. . . ."

The newspaperman came under the shading porch and said, "A lot of people feel Delavan was behind it."

"Who else could it be?"

"Some of the ranchers have mixed feelings about it." Packard, out of the Great Lakes state of Michigan, was a bearded, flap-eared youth with an engaging manner. The brown suit, though above average in quality, had seen its best days, but to offset its eastern cut he wore cowboy boots and a western hat that had never seen a drop of water. "Would one of you gentlemen be Crowheart?"

Reluctantly Johnny flicked an acknowledging finger against the brim of his hat. More and more, as the morning wore on and edged into noon, this worried notion that he was being watched kept hammering at Crowheart. Ever since stepping out here he'd been checking off the passersby, and other activity along the street. It wasn't that far to the bluffs fringing on the northern edges of Medora; within Winchester range, he figured. Or one of the Morgan brothers or someone else could be lurking in a nearby building. When they'd called out Big Mike Delavan this morning, Johnny had known right off Delavan was telling the truth despite the man's sorrowful reputation.

"Yes, well, could I talk to you in private?"

"Suppose we could mosey back inside," Johnny said, somewhat anxious to be getting under shelter again.

As Johnny moved ahead of the editor back into Genial Jim's, sunlight sparked a dull edge off of a rifle barrel being withdrawn from an upper window of a building downstreet. The man holding the rifle was Odie Blaine, proud to be a member of Turk Widen's bunch, left behind to prove he could do killing when it called for that. Somewhat nettled that he hadn't gotten a clear shot at some shiftless cowpoke named Crowheart, Odie Blaine set the rifle leaning against the wall. All of them, the Morgan brothers, Yakima, and those he rode with, had left this morning for the northern reaches of the Badlands, that Missouri River country.

He had spotted Crowheart stabling his horse and tailed him over to Genial Jim's, where the outlaw had surveyed the street and decided that a dry goods store opposite was the place to wait until the waddy reappeared. It had been an easy matter to sneak in the back entrance and come up to the storeroom on the second floor. A couple of times the merchant had come up to get supplies, with Odie Blaine sneaking in behind some cider barrels. Tired of sitting on a keg he'd dragged over, the outlaw stood up and shuffled over and scooped some dried apples out of an open barrel. He hadn't asked why they wanted this cowpoke bushwhacked, nor did he care a whole lot. He just wanted to prove to Turk Widen that he could kill when asked, or do any other crooked job. He had one notch on his Navy Colt: a drunken gambler.

Over at Genial Jim's, editor Packard seated at a back table with Johnny Crowheart, said, "Big Mike Delavan has been nothing but trouble for Medora. Yet you feel he didn't kill Ripley."

"More or less."

"I've the feeling you're holding something back, Mr. Crowheart."

"Look, Packard, I feel bad enough about this. If I hadn't let them talk me into going over to Little Misery, Mort Ripley would still be alive."

"You must understand, Mr. Crowheart, that as an editor I must ask the sometimes painful questions. It's my job to dig for the facts . . . and the truth."

"The truth"—Johnny rose from the chair—"wouldn't help Ripley now." His temper frayed, he shouldered out a side entrance and cut back alongside the two-story frame building. What he needed was mind-clearing air, which he could only find astride a horse.

He found that some forty minutes later south along the river, below a cut bank shielding him from the sun, and atop it, sedge grass for his horse. An avid fisherman, he always had in his saddlebag some fish hooks and line and a little dried jerky he used for bait. Cutting down a slender willow branch to use as a pole, he rigged it, then cast the baited hook out into the waters eddying peacefully around a sandbar. Though he caught some walleyed pike, Johnny released them as he considered packing up his possibles upon returning to the Hashknife and trying Wyoming again.

Only when sunbeams were dimming away did Crowheart venture back along the Little Missouri and into town again. He lingered at the stable, where he'd again spend the night since no rooms were available. To pass the time, Johnny curried his horse. He would miss Pearly Gate, for his mind was now set on leaving, Carrie Morgan or not. His hanging around would only bring down the wrath of her brothers and Ezra Morgan. She was special, alien to what the rest of that clan believed in, more important to him even than Pearly Gate or a new saddle.

"Shucks," he said bitterly, "no sense just dreaming about what could have been." It was time, he mused, to tell the bossman his intentions.

Dousing the coal oil lamp, he ambled over to the front door and opened it to hear a rifle cut loose. The first bullet struck the metal door latch churning sparks from it and peppering Crowheart's hand. In rapid succession the ambusher spiked the door with slugs as Crowheart spun around and dove back into the livery stable, but not before noting the rifle spouting flame from an alleyway upstreet. Scrambling to his feet, Johnny hurried past a horse rearing in its stall and went head first through an open window to land in some weeds. He was a lot angrier than he'd been this morning after finding out about Ripley. Determined to find out who was behind this, he recklessly dashed out into the street and unleathered his gun as he angled toward the alley. The ambusher caught a glimpse of Crowheart closing in and fired. Then Johnny's handgun responded, chipping wood away from the corner of the building and driving the rifleman away.

Running into the alley, Johnny finally made out the ambusher about to turn onto the street to the east, only to hesitate when several men came into view, and he headed back Johnny's way, discarding the rifle and pulling out his handgun.

Crouching, Johnny triggered his own weapon first, two or three times—he couldn't recall which—and the ambusher veered clumsily and fell against wall, then went to his knees. His gun belched bluish flame, a wild shot that struck a barrel. Crowheart responded by pumping two more slugs into the ambusher. The man folded over and lay still.

Now Johnny was aware of others coming in behind him, and that he was trembling, the pain in his hand forgotten, for it dawned on him that he'd just killed his first man. When someone asked him what had happened, he said dazily, "He tried killing me just as I left that livery stable."

The crowd drifted over to the dead man, and it was T.O. Addison who toed the body onto its back and said, "A hardcase; but one I've never seen before."

"Could be the same man who killed Ripley?"

"I'll bet that's it."

Jake Murdock pushed through those pressing around Crowheart and draped a hand on his shoulder. "Did he wing you, Johnny?"

"He tried, but no, I'm okay. Just shaken up, some."

The Badlands Cowboy editor, Packard, appeared and, after glancing at the body, came over. "Trouble seems to follow you around, Mr. Crowheart. But that's one less outlaw we have to worry about. I heard someone ask if that's the man who killed Mort Ripley. Is it, Mr. Crowheart?"

"It probably is," said Kile Sandby. "He could have been over at Big Mike's when that pool game was going on. Knew that Crowheart, here, and Ripley had some money on them."

"I still say Big Mike is behind this," claimed Addison.

"Maybe so, Addison, but without any proof we'll have to let it go." Jake Murdock waited with Johnny until the crowd began flowing away. "I expect you still didn't get a room."

"Guess my luck's been bad of late."

"Here's the key to my room over at the Rough Riders Hotel. Head up there and get cleaned up, and if you've got a mind to sack out, do so."

And that's just what Crowheart did, despite his not having had supper, and upon arriving up in the rancher's room, he stretched out and fell asleep almost immediately. He awoke once, around eleven, he thought, and listened to the sound of fireworks decorating the night sky over Medora. But wearied by all that had happened, he chose the bed instead of a late meal or a saloon.

They buried Mort Ripley that Sunday morning on Gravestone Bluff. Except for the Baptist minister reading a final prayer from his bible and Arthur Pack-

131

ard, none of the townspeople showed up. But standing hatless among the grave markers were the cowboys and those ranchers who'd attended the Stockmen's meeting.

"The Lord giveth . . . and the Lord taketh away . . ."

At the concluding words of the minister the grave digger began shoveling reddish soil down onto the pine box, and everyone began moving off the bluff toward his horse. A hand tugged at Johnny's arm, and then Darin Murdock spoke to him.

"Crowheart, my father told me why you came with him."

"That so," he said crossly.

"I see Bill Lowman's hand in this," went on Darin Murdock, a sandy-haired youth just turned twenty. "Lowman probably told you that I'd gotten into trouble back east. I did, Crowheart. That's why I'm home. Never did take to ranching much."

"He mentioned that."

"Lowman has a way of not leaving too much out." Darin smiled. "I, well, when I got back I hung around Medora for a few days. Mostly doing a lot of self-pitying thinking. Did some drinking, too. Strange that I should run into the Morgan brothers over at Little Misery. But, considering they're our neighbors, and unfriendly ones at that, I got to talking to them."

"Murdock," he said curtly, "I'd appreciate your getting to the point of all this—"

"What I'm trying to say, Crowheart, is that I intend to buckle down when I get out to the ranch, prove to my father that I can cut the mustard."

"You know what's strange, Murdock, that Joe Bob

132

knew I was over at that billiard parlor."

"Some buffalo hunter named Yakima Pierce came into that saloon and told us about seeing you going down the street. Next thing I know, Joe Bob and his brothers cut out of there. They did mention something about your sparking their sister, Carrie. Seems you still don't believe me."

Reaching his horse, Johnny untied the reins from the pole fence strung around the cemetery and climbed into the saddle. "It did seem strange you keeping company with the Morgans . . . and the others with them who had the look of longriders. After what's happened I just don't know what to believe."

"Guess I was too drunk to notice," Darin Murdock said lamely. "But from now on I'll be darned careful who I drink with."

And, mused Johnny Crowheart, I'm going to be watching my backtrail. It was more than coincidence that ambusher going for him. It had also served to change his mind about quitting the Hashknife. Spurring after the Murdocks and Bucky O'Connor, Johnny knew now that the son of Jake Murdock was mixed up in something. There was an old saying that a man should bring his enemies closer than his friends, which was what Darin was trying to do to him. There was Carrie Morgan and maybe the promise of knowing her better. There was this loyalty to a rancher who'd befriended a cowpoke down on his luck. Besides, good riding jobs were kind of scarce in Wyoming, too.

Chapter Ten

In the northwest corner of the Badlands the Missouri River gorged past Crow Fly High Hill and then ox-bowed to the east. The wide river was near flood stage, treacherous with undercurrents and bearing the carcasses of a few dead animals and flotsam. Before the Great Northern Railroad laid track north of the river, it was the riverboat that linked the wheat-stubbed fields of the Midwest with the Northwest territories. One of the legacies left behind were the shacks of the woodcutters scattered in coves and gullies opening onto the river breaks. These old deserted woodyards marked by big cottonwood stumps and rotting buildings made natural hideouts for the longriders.

Westward a few miles, the Yellowstone mouthed into the Missouri, while north of this watery conjunction lay Fort Buford, an abandoned army post. Further to the north, the Badlands ended near the Canadian border.

"No sense trailing them outlaws in there."

From a crumbly ledge, a small rock kicked loose by rancher John Keller's horse went tumbling downslope toward a creek flooding a coulee bottom. Bitter experience told the rancher the outlaws they'd been trailing since late yesterday had made good their escape into the breaks and that he'd just lost around thirty horses. Only last week two of his cowhands living out of a line shack had seen one of them killed in a running gun battle with other outlaws. That time these outlaws had gotten away with over a hundred head of cattle. Reluctantly he told his men they were heading back to the home ranch as he reined around and headed south. A rancher could only take so much of this rustling before he went belly-up. All because of the many outlaw gangs infesting the Missouri breaks and deeper in the Badlands, men who used to do their thieving at night were now so emboldened that some rustled cattle in broad daylight. Sunk in his despairing thoughts, the rancher failed to notice the light reflecting from the rim of Crow Fly High Hill.

The lookout shoved the field glass back into a saddlebag and rode down the northern flank of the hill. As Yakima had told them, cattlemen were hesitant about looking for outlaws in the dangerous recesses of the breaks. Maybe, pondered George Ramshorn, this was going to work out after all. Ramshorn was a big, brooding man out of Idaho. His specialty was the running iron. He was what lawmen called derisively a brand artist; for Ramshorn could create an effective imitation of an established brand with a cinch-ring heated in a fire and held with the tips of two sticks, or he could deftly alter an existing brand to one more to his liking. Sometimes he would use a camp cook's pot-hook to shape a brand, and since a man could be arrested up here for carrying a running-iron tied to his saddle, brand blotter Ramshorn merely resorted to carrying a short one in his warbag. However, for the time being his running-iron would stay in his warbag, for the deal worked out by Turk Widen was to sell any horses or cattle they rustled to those coming down from Medicine Hat.

These were some French and English half-breeds called the Metis. Their leader, Louis Riel, had been involved in the Red River Rebellion against the Dominion of Canada, and after this was resolved, but not to the liking of the Metis or Riel, the half-breed fled to Montana. It was here, Turk Widen had told them, he'd run into Louis Riel, who later was asked by his fellow Metis to lead a new rebellion up in Saskatchewan. To help finance this new uprising, they had struck this deal with Widen that he furnish them with rustled cattle and horses. They didn't even have to drive the livestock across the border, which was oftentimes when rustlers got caught by vengeful cattlemen or law officers.

It took George Ramshorn most of the sunlight hours to work his way back through the breaks composed of knife-edged ridges, creeks and draws lowering toward the Missouri. Deer were plentiful, so much so that the outlaw had to resist the urge to unsheath his Winchester 50-96 express; one shot would not only fetch back those cowpunchers but see Turk Widen ragging him for his carelessness. And, he scared up a lobo wolf still muffed in winter's heavy, grey-furred coat. Around him the many trees were leafing, the ground sucking in spring runoff. Brush grew thick in the coulees, and Ramshorn relaxed a little when he encountered a cottonwood split by lightning. Then he brought his bronc along a narrow draw, which widened after a short ride to come onto a grassy area littered with stumps boned by age and beyond, three cabins straddling the high riverbank. He glimpsed Kelly Bartow showing himself on a ledge. There were two corrals: the one Yakima Pierce had enlarged, and the smaller roping corral where he turned his horse loose to have it mingle with others they rode.

With his rifle hanging loosely in one hand, Ramshorn stepped over to the middle cabin and said, "Like you expected, Yakima, they turned back." Idling on the porch along with Yakima were Widen and Mack Blackthorn.

Turk Widen shaped a pleased smile. "You done good, Yakima, picking this layout." While still in territorial prison over in Montana, there had been some communication with the buffalo hunter, and Widen sent Yakima Pierce up to Medicine Hat to confer with the Metis, and their leader, Louis Riel. Since Riel had told them he would take all the livestock they could rustle, Widen held a powwow with the leaders of other outlaw gangs, some of them camping out in places like this and a few in the Badlands. They had no choice but to agree to Widen's terms; otherwise it meant a long and risky cattle drive.

On the front porch of another cabin two of the Morgan brothers were arguing about something, and he supposed Joe Bob was sleeping off a drunk. They weren't all that good at working cattle; but they knew the country, and he planned to use their homestead as a sort of relay station. Chiefly, Turk Widen craved not a drink but a woman. He turned his bored eyes upon Yakima Pierce sprawled on the bench with his dirty flannel shirt stretched over that kettle-belly. The man was using his hunting knife to carve meat from a big soup bone. Widen could feel some hunger pangs.

"Who's cookin' tonight?"

"Bartow."

"Abe," Widen called out, "get up there and spell Kelly at guard duty."

"It ain't time yet, Turk."

"Just do it," he said pleasantly.

As Abe Morgan grabbed his rifle and began trudging back into the trees, Yakima Pierce tossed the bone away and said, "I hope Riel don't disappoint us."

Widen smiled. "He needs us more'n we need him. Think of it; Louis Riel's trying to take over a whole section of Canada. Man's got grit."

"Speaking of grit, think them Morgans will have the stomach for what's to come?"

"Too late to back out now."

Mack Blackthorn spun the cylinder of the handgun he'd been cleaning and said, "How's this breed gonna find this place?"

"Riel's been through here before, on his way to Montana." Widen cast an idle glance at the darkening sky. "Could be he'll show up today."

But it was the following evening that the Metis ghosted into camp, fifteen men fanning out and sitting quietly and eerily on their horses as the outlaws looked questioningly at Turk Widen. Then another horseman appeared and rode over to the larger corral as Widen strolled after him, and reining his horse around, Louis Riel, a dark-faced man with black bushy hair poking out around a fur cap, said somberly, "So, only thirty head in there, Turk. I expected more from you."

"Got more, Riel. Got another hundred head hidden

in a box canyon."

"Cattle?"

"Don't fret about that either, Louis. Expect you'll be a-wanting to camp here tonight. We've got venison and beef and the fixings, and whiskey if you crave that. And a darned good plan worked out that'll profit both of us."

Nodding around the scowl, Louis Riel barked a command in French to his men as he slid to the ground. He began unsaddling his horse. "So, Turk, let's hear about this . . . grandiose plan. . . ."

"First of all, I've got someone right in with the cattlemen, who will tell me just where they'll be summering their cattle. No sense beating them Badlands for cattle now. Let them ranchers do all the hard work. Once they get their cattle to summering in scattered herds, it'll be just a matter of rustling one herd after another. Expect some cowpokes'll get killed. But that's good, too, 'cause it'll put the devil's fear into the rest. What I'm thinking now is, Riel, how'd you plan to get these horses across the Missouri flooded as it is?"

"My men are very resourceful."

"Contacted some other outlaw gangs about bringing the cattle they rustle up here. Plenty of canyons to hold them until you show up."

"So, Monsieur Widen, there is your price—"

"For sure a man's got to make a profit," laughed Widen.

Ma foi! To be sure."

"First, let's chow down, Louis. I feel good about this. There's more cattle down there than the Badlands can handle. More than me and my men can ever

140

rustle. And heaps of wild horses. Both of us stand to get what we want out of this."

It was the Morgan brothers vanguarding the Widen gang southeasterly away from the Missouri River and through the Badlands. The route taken by the heavily-armed men carried them past Yellowstone Point Cemetery and some ranches to the south spread along Charbonneau Creek. Turk Widen wanted to avoid, if possible, encountering any line riders, even though he knew most of the cowpunchers working on the scattered ranches were involved in the spring roundup.

Southwesterly, a rain shower came out of black-bellied clouds, while another cloud bank drifting just north of them was disgorging rainwater. In between these clouds the high domed sky was clear. It wasn't that far to the Morgan place, and being in no hurry, Widen let his horse jiggle along with the others. The deal struck with the Metis, Widen thought smugly, would see both of them making a profit. He felt good about that, and of being an outlaw and just drifting whenever the mood fancied him. Now he had to smile at the way Yakima Pierce rode, sitting humpbacked, those long legs thrust into lengthened stirrups almost brushing the ground, and at the grim set to Yakima's face as if the man still had visions of sighting another herd of buffer. He was a strange one, old Yakima, having thoughts contrary to the other outlaws. That skinning job the man had done on that waddy down in Medora spoke a warning to Turk Widen to never fully trust Yakima Pierce. Would he have the stomach to do that? Nope, not if he wanted to sleep nights.

Clean-cut killing with a gun suited Widen just fine, and he glanced down at the 1875 Sharps 50-90 reposing in a fringed leather sheath tied to Yakima's saddle, the famous Big Fifty. From stories told him by other buffalo and hide hunters, an elk or big bull buffalo never twitched a muscle after catching a slug from that Sharps. And he was anxious to see Yakima put it to use, wanting to bet a slug from it could pierce the thick steel hide of a Northern Pacific locomotive.

"Odie Blaine should be waiting for us at the Morgans," Mack interrupted Turk's reverie.

"He should be, Mack. Though I still have second thoughts about getting rid of that waddy . . . Crowheart."

"He could have spilled the beans about that rancher's son hookin' up with us," said Mack Blackthorn. "I hear Crowheart sure had the hots for that Morgan girl." He said that just to see Joe Bob's reaction and grinned tightly as Morgan twisted in the saddle and flung back an angry grimace.

"Easy, Mack," Widen said quietly. "We need these sodbusters."

"Sure, but afterward I want to see just what Joe Bob is made of."

"Yakima," Turk Widen said, "you haven't uttered a word all day. Was Kelly Bartow's cooking all that bad?"

"I've had worse. I still think those Metis should have altered the brands on those horses. Plumb carelessness."

"They probably will. I've got to hand it to you the way you set up this rustling thing. Handled right, we should make a bundle out of this."

"Just so nobody messes up. Another skinning job would sure whet my appetite."

As a butte called Stony Johnny fell behind, Joe Bob Morgan motioned to a wide draw passing between two hills. "That's Caprock." Then he jogged ahead of the others and down into a coulee fed by a creek and lush with trees and underbrush. Ahead, the outlaws could see a sod house built into the wall of the coulee and assorted smaller buildings and a corral. The low baying of a coon dog and that of a setter welcomed the riders. Down by the creek some hogs were wallowing in the mud, and they scattered chickens picking at seeds strewn on the barren patch of ground by the buildings. Three horses in the corral whickered a greeting, and even a jackass stalled in a rickety shed thrust its head out the door, but wolfer Ezra Morgan made no attempt to rise from the shaded porch of the house.

"We're home, Pa," said Abe Morgan.

"Boy, I ain't blind."

"Did Odie Blaine show up?"

"Just me and Carrie is here. Who in tarnation is this Blaine?"

"One of Widen's men."

"That big ugly gent wearin' the buffer coat?"

"That's Yakima Pierce."

"Outlaws," Ezra Morgan spat out. "I suppose you expect me to feed this bunch, Abe. If so, they'll pay — hard Yankee coin."

"We'll be right pleased to do that," said Turk Widen as he stepped over and Abe Morgan wheeled his horse

143

around and brought it to the corral. "Nice place you've got here. Fingering a doeskin coin bag out of a vest pocket, Widen took out several silver dollars. "This'll pay for what chow we eat, Mr. Morgan, and for your keeping quiet about us being here."

"T'aint enough! Not hardly enough. From the size of that buffer hunter, the man can eat a side of beef hisself at one setting."

An engaging smile on his face, Widen stepped onto the porch and settled into a wooden chair. He removed his dusty hat and hooked it on a knee crossed over the other one. "This is going to be a long and profitable summer for all of us."

"Rustling, I take it."

"That's right, Ezra, right as rain."

"You talk my sons into this foolishness?"

"Your sons, Mr. Morgan, came to a mutual agreement with Yakima."

"Widen, I thought you was ramrodding this outfit," he said scornfully.

"Make no mistake about it, Ezra, I've killed before . . . and will do so again. There are a lot of men involved, outlaws and otherwise, on both sides of the border. Big money's involved here, too. What you get should help you fix this place up, and leave some for your aging years. But cross me, Mr. Morgan, and you'll die." The smile widened. "But I know it won't come to that, not a-tall."

Ezra Morgan unleashed a stream of tobacco juice that splattered off the porch railing. In his eyes burned resentment and also greed for the money the outlaw kept clinking in his left hand. "Make no mistake about this either, Mr. Outlaw. You need me more than I need you. I got no love for them thievin' ranchers either. The other thing is, and there'll be no mistake about this, you and your men keep your hands off'n my daughter. That happens, this old Remington of mine's going into action."

Alongside the creek but this side of it grew a large garden, perhaps a good half-acre in size, which was screened from the house by thorny underbrush. It was here that Turk Widen glanced when a young woman appeared and hurried toward the side door of the house. The last woman Widen had bedded was that bar girl down at Marmarth, a woman who could never hold a candle to one of such unexpected youth and beauty as to bring a wanting catch into his throat. Sunlight lancing through the trees did tricks with Carrie Morgan's raven hair even though it was pinned up, and then she was in the house, leaving the outlaw still staring. He pondered as Johnny Crowheart and other cowpokes had done, just how could a man such as Ezra Morgan, with his windburned skin stretched taut across his bony face and sour disposition, sire a daughter like that. She could have been orphaned out, a notion which he discarded.

"My daughter'll do the cooking, Widen. But tend to your own laundering. Now, let's get down to the tap root as to what I should get out of this."

Chapter Eleven

By the first week of June the ranchers forming the Little Missouri roundup had worked their way from Box Elder Creek on the Little Missouri to Big Beaver and up that stream until they would encounter men from the Yellowstone roundup. The long days in the saddle began with the cook rousting the hands out around three in the morning, and after a hasty breakfast of coffee, fat pork, biscuits and beans, the captain of the roundup, Bill Lowman, sang out:

"Alright, boys, catch your horses!"

Since hovering near the warming fire caused them to spend the day afoot, they hurried over to where the night wrangler was driving the saddle band into a rope corral rigged up by stretching some ropes between the wheels of the mess and bedroll wagons. One of the best ropers, Arty Lamar of the Hashknife, had been selected to do the morning roping, and he picked out a horse for each waddy who then saddled it, the horses dancing or bucking or whickering their displeasure. In a little while, some forty cowhands awaited orders from the captain, while a dozen others prepared to drive the day herd to the new camping ground.

Quickly segundo Bill Lowman divided the forty riders into two bands. "Wilmot," he said to Wilmot Dow of the Elkhorn Spread, "you take this bunch and work about fifteen miles out on this side of Big Beaver. And, Parsons, take the others thataway." And then Lowman rode to the new campsite, to supervise the branding crew and be there when cattle were brought in.

Johnny Crowheart was in the bunch splashing across Big Beaver. This morning he was mounted on a grulla he'd named Sidewinder, since the bronc had a habit of fighting the reins at times while trying to buck sideways, but otherwise it gave him little trouble. Sidewinder, as was Crowheart, was leaned by the arduous work. The morning work was called circle riding, meaning that as his riders go out, Bylo Parsons would detach men from time to time to have them search out certain sections of the range for cattle, until finally those farthest away came in searching on lines that tended to a common center as of an open fan.

After Johnny had dropped away with Ike Walton, they began searching between soapstone buttes for cattle, in pockets, basins, and coulees, which were covered with dense patches of brushwood or windbeaten trees. It was still dark when they began scaring up cattle, which bolted in the direction of Big Beaver, some seven miles away. There were no fences in the Badlands: thus cattle from the various ranches mingled together over the long winters: longhorns, shorthorn bulls and angus.

Still riding with Johnny was that Medora incident, one man dead by his hand, and another done away so brutally. When learning of it, the Hashknife waddies treated him with a quiet cordiality, as if by killing a man he'd been set apart. Bill Lowman had spoken to him about this, telling Crowheart that while driving trail herds up from Texas he'd been forced to kill three men; two Comanches and a Jayhawker. "It never goes away," he'd told Crowheart, "just dims some. Sooner or later every cowpoke faces the same situation, the lucky ones not having to kill a man." He had kept secret from Lowman the presence of Darin Murdock over in Little Misery. During the roundup, Darin hadn't proven himself much of a hand with a rope; so he'd been assigned the job of running errands for the captain, and if he resented this, Darin Murdock gave no indication.

As the haze of night lifted, there could still be seen in low spots smoky wisps of mist. The faraway booming of a rifle startled Crowheart, until he realized it was probably rancher Teddy Roosevelt bringing down a deer or elk. He had gotten to know the man better around the late-night campfires, learning that Roosevelt was quite a politician back in New York. Also, that the rancher could play a practical joke on someone with the best of them. Despite his worries about Darin Murdock being involved with those outlaws, and his mooning about Carrie Morgan among other things, Johnny was enjoying himself.

Now the cattle Johnny and Walton had chased out of the rough and sometimes all but impassable terrain surged to join others being herded toward Big Beaver Creek. The sun was rimming out over the Killdeer Mountains fringing eastward on the Badlands. "Ike, think we missed any?"

"It's like going fishing, Johnny boy, you never catch them all."

"Sounds like Roosevelt's got something."

"That'll sure set well with me."

"If it was him . . ."

He rode closer to Crowheart. "I see you're still spooked over what happened down at Medora. You flash money around that town or Little Misery, someone's bound to want it. Outlaws, I mean. Medora is pretty safe, but that other place isn't gonna see this cowpoke goin' into it."

"Guess I didn't use good judgement by taking on Big Mike."

"It's hurrah for your taking his measure. But just remember that Yakima Pierce ain't forgotten it was me putting another knot in his head when he came at you with that knife. And that I bested him at poker."

"Meanin' it was Yakima skinning poor old Ripley?"

"Gotta be, Johnny."

"What worries me is that he's mixed up with the Morgan brothers."

Gently Ike Walton said, "Maybe you should forget that Carrie gal. Her pa just plumb hates us waddies . . . and that's a fact."

"Maybe so. I still wonder why I didn't draw my time."

"Wondering ain't gonna get these cattle over to Big Beaver. Over there amongst those willows, there's some longhorns."

After a while, riding onto an elevation, Johnny drew up in wonderment at the Badlands shrugging away shadows from its sun-dusted buttes. Down by Big Beaver, cattle from both sides of the creek were being hazed by other cowhands toward a wide plain alongside the twisting stream, where the day herd was being kept. The two wagons were just pulling into camp, but already the branding crew had its fire going and was working on the first bunches of cattle that had arrived. A rapid count by Johnny of the cattle coming in showed around a thousand head would have to be branded and ear-notched, calfs and mavericks. He could see Bill Lowman, with his tally book and astride his horse, presiding over the sort of frenzied activity in camp. It wouldn't take more'n a quarter of an hour for cook Woody Hannagan to have a fire going and dinner cooking over it. Also there was the OX Spread cook, a gimpy-legged oldtimer named Jingles, helping out. Once the noon meal was over with, they would set up a Sibley tent Roosevelt had brought along, a circular tent with a stove in the middle where some of the waddies slept, to the derisive smiles and jokes of others.

The creek bottom ran back to sandstone cliffs tinged with black coal seams and layers of burned clay, and the air was calm and warming. Under the watchful eye of the day wrangler, the saddle horses not being used were kept separated from the cattle. Those cowboys who'd just arrived with bunches of cattle kept them apart from the day herd, the calves and mavericks in it having already been branded. To the lowing of a cow, a rider would cut out a calf and rope it by its hind legs, or drag it over to the branding team. For the branding a large corral had been erected. Now a bulldogger and a flanker would hold down the calf as the roper called out the brand on the cow to tallyman Bill Lowman. While the calf was being held down, the brander would pick out the brand worn by the calf's mother, and after he had burned the brand into the calf's flank, the butcher would dewmark an ear and either slip the severed part of ear into his pocket as a tally or pass it to the tallyman. Then, if the calf was male, he was usually castrated and the fries thrown into a pile. These might be cooked and enjoyed later. Tending the fire and branding irons this morning was Darin Murdock, whose cry of hot iron seemed to ring out constantly. After a while Crowheart and Walton took their turns with the branding team.

Around nooning all of the circle riders had come in bringing more cattle, and while some ate hurriedly, other waddies were holding these cattle in a compact bunch. Afterward, when the noon meal was over, a couple of riders from each of the five ranches sharing the Little Missouri roundup began the cutting process. A difficult chore, not only for the man cutting out cattle marked with his brand, but since the cattle were always stirring about, even more so for a cutting horse. And always there were some animals breaking out; immediately two waddies would swing out after it and lane the steer back into the milling herd. When separated, the cattle formed a new herd of that particular ranch.

Long after the sun had set the work went on. Tiredly some of the men clustered near the cook wagon to have Woody Hannagan heap their tin plates with hot food. Only when Bill Lowman gave the word did the work for the day cease, and the bob-tail guard was sent out to watch the cattle as the others sought their bedrolls and what sleep they could get.

With his head propped up on his saddle and still wearing his hat to keep away some of the night chill, Johnny eased around in his bedroll until he got comfortable. He was one of those sleeping out in the open, sometimes staring, as others were, at the light glowing from the stove in that Sibley tent. Shortly after sundown Bill Lowman had asked him quietly if he'd seen Darin Murdock, and he'd told Lowman that he hadn't. After his segundo had gone away, Johnny couldn't help wondering what mischief Jake's son was up to this time, since Darin Murdock had a careless habit of wandering away from camp at times without the captain's permission. Only the night critters were out roaming now—coyotes and wolfs and night hawks—and pondered Johnny, perhaps some outlaws. Yesterday word had been brought by a passing cowhand that a herd of Rocking V cattle out toward Wibaux had been rustled, and other ranchers had reported missing some of their horses. As for Darin Murdock, Crowheart had been cordial but kept his distance. Sometimes the kid, as he called Darin, could be real mean to his horse or take out his displeasure on one of the Hashknife waddies. Once Johnny had caught Darin staring at his father out of hate-glittering eyes, and a chill had gone through him, as the hate-filled stare was followed by an angelic smile for the man who'd sired him. It had gotten so that whenever Johnny found himself alone during roundup as he scoured the Badlands for cattle, there was a part of him that kept looking for the kid or even Yakima Pierce. More and more it became wedged in his mind that Darin Murdock was up to some devious ploy. He'd gotten to buddying up to the other ranchers, too—Roosevelt, O'Connor, the others—something that troubled Crowheart to the extent he just might have to tell Bill Lowman all that had taken place over at Little Misery.

"You asleep?"

"Trying to get there."

"Johnny, you ever seen so many stars. . . ."

"Nope; awful awesome sparkling thataway."

Sleepily Ike Walton said, "Saw more stars than this when I tried riding Widow Maker last summer. Now, I'll tell you, that . . ."

As his eyes lidded over, and Walton droned on, Johnny was grateful that he didn't have the graveyard shift, the worst of the watches since a waddy had to watch the cattle from midnight until two in the morning and never really get a good night's sleep. And somewhat happy about that, he fell asleep.

"Took a long time finding you, Murdock."

"You found me, Trace. Did you bring the money?"

"What Turk Widen gave me." He passed to the other rider a leather pouch, which Darin Murdock opened.

"It better be what we agreed on."

Sniffling, and then wiping his nose with the back of a gloved hand, Trace Morgan said, "I didn't take none, if that's what you're getting at."

"Appears that it's all here." Moonlight beaming over his shoulder revealed the sudden smile Darin had for the sodbuster scowling back. "It won't be until next week before we hook up with the Yellowstone roundup. I just hope Widen hasn't planned anything

154

until we split up and head back to our home ranges. You come alone?"

He waved a vague hand. "Yakima's out there someplace."

"Yakima? After what he did to that cowpoke down in Medora, I thought Widen would keep him under a tight leash." His anger fanned his eyes into narrowed slits.

Trace Morgan giggled as he slapped a hand down at his horse's neck. "That was something what Yakima did to the waddy. I tell you, he's a pure artist with that hunting knife. He came along a-purpose."

"You tell Yakima not to try anything now. It'll ruin what I'm setting up. And you tell Turk that Odie Blaine got gunned down. It seems Crowheart was a shade better with a gun. But I still want Crowheart taken care of. Later, after we get back to the Hashknife. There's over fifty cowpunchers not counting the ranchers back there at Big Beaver. Tell Yakima that."

"It'll pleasure me doing that, Murdock. How about a cowpoke named Ike Walton, is he there, too?"

"Walton's there. Someone else Yakima has a grudge against?"

"Yakima's all full of hate and strange ideas. Same's you, Mr. Murdock."

"Damn you, Trace. I've got my own reasons for doing this. And none of them concern you in the least. Did the Metis show up?"

"Bought all them horses we rustled. Want more, and all the cattle we can get. Strange people, but long's they got money, Turk Widen don't care. Or me and my brothers. Soon's I get enough silver dollars, it's long gone south for this old turkey buzzard." He giggled again, then took another swipe at his runny nose.

From an inner pocket, Darin Murdock fished out a folded piece of paper, and he said firmly, "See that Turk gets this. It's a map detailing just where those ranchers are going to summer their cattle. I've spent some time over at these ranches before spring roundup spying out the best routes in and out."

"My brothers and I have been doin' some snooping ourselves. We've got a pretty good idea of the terrain. This is gonna be some fun summer, riding with Turk Widen's bunch."

"Don't lose that map, now. And, Trace, you tell Yakima to hold back until roundup is over. Now, git."

When a hand touched Johnny Crowheart's shoulder and a low-pitched voice reached out to him, the one irritating thought he had was that Ike Walton was still rambling on about that bucking horse, Widow Maker, but upon opening his eyes he discovered it to be an Elkhorn waddy, who said tiredly, "Cocktail guard time, Johnny."

"Yeah," he mumbled sleepily, "I hear you." Quickly he scrambled out of his bedroll and yawned away his tired feeling as he rolled up the bedroll and headed for his horse standing unsaddled with others along the picket line. The cooks were already up, etched in the glow of their campfire as they prepared the morning meal. After saddling his horse, then tying his bedroll behind the saddle and donning his sheepskin, he had barely enough time to gulp down a scalding hot cup

156

of coffee before riding away chomping on a hunk of fat pork. Other cowpokes were coming in or going out to the vast herd stretched along the wide flood plain below the dark sandstone cliffs.

Riding around the perimeter of the herd, as were others, he knew this would be a longer day because of his getting up earlier. Somehow he didn't mind a whole heap because in another week or less—they were told by the ranchers also along on the roundup—they would be hooking up with the Yellowstone bunch. Then, after returning to the home range, there'd be time for some of them to hightail it into town and see the elephant and otherwise celebrate. But had the young waddy been aware of the chilling fact that Yakima Pierce was just to the west of them holed up and waiting for a chance to commit murder, there would be no soft whistle coming from his lips as he let the vision of Carrie Morgan help pass away the few lonely hours until another day broke over the Badlands.

Chapter Twelve

Another three days found the Hashknife and others involved in the Little Missouri roundup far to the southwest on Big Beaver Creek. The weather had held; just a few scattered rain showers and a steady wind which always seemed to gust through the Badlands. The day herd had grown steadily larger, making Jake Murdock remark somewhat worriedly that he might have to cut out some cattle for shipping, which was generally done in the fall when the cattle were slick from summer grazing.

Monday came, with the wind coming in stronger than usual, even at dawning. This hadn't stopped Bill Lowman from sending out the waddies to look for cattle, as he knew sometime today they might connect with the other ranchers bringing their herds in from the west. He, among others, would be glad to get back to the home range. He had also taken the responsibility of captaining the roundup in stride. The only sour spots were these nightly jaunts taken by Darin Murdock. He'd tried talking to Jake's son and found that the boy had become a man, one with a sullen hatred for his father. How did you fire the boss's son? Maybe challenging young Murdock to a fist fight was the answer—try to knock some sense into him. Or maybe it might pry out the reason he hated his father. Perhaps he could explain to Darin that under Jake Murdock's crusty and abrupt exterior there was a man who truly loved his ranch and son. No, he mustn't mettle in this, at least not for the moment. Behind him came dust billowing from the wagons and day herd heading upstream toward another campsite.

About twelve miles farther to the southwest, cowhands were fanning out in search of cattle. Down into a draw rode Crowheart. Yesterday he had slipped while bulldogging a calf and twisted his ankle, with the slight injury not keeping him from the saddle. On the elevations the wind was kicking up dust, which filmed his clothing and came stinging to the eyes. It had warmed into the high eighties, the sky a metallic blue overhead and dust-hazed along the horizon. Most of the ranchers were wanting it to rain, fearing another hot and dry summer as had happened the last two years.

In the draw he came upon a shorthorn bull and kiyeed it through the leafy underbrush and upward toward other cattle he and Ike Walton had found. He looked around for Walton, and called out, but only the shrilling wind answered Crowheart. Distantly, about a half mile, he spotted a couple of waddies hazing the cattle they'd come upon streamward. Johnny knew that the opposite way other cowhands would be doing the same thing. For a while he lazed behind the cattle, waiting for his partner. They were only a couple of miles from Big Beaver, the morning coming onto noon, and still Ike Walton hadn't appeared. Walton's horse could have thrown a shoe, or going down one of those treacherous slopes after some cattle he could have been thrown, with his horse wandering off. As the other waddies angled their cattle closer to Johnny, he cut their way.

"Walton got himself lost back there."

"Maybe he stopped to take a nap," suggested a hand.

"That could be it." Johnny joined in their laughter.

"Go ahead, Johnny, we'll see these cattle get in."

He swung Pearly Gate around and cantered back to where they'd been working the draws and coulees. He passed through the draw where he'd hazed out that shorthorn bull and back to where they'd separated. Walton had gone deeper to the south and down amongst thick brush and trees choking a coulee. Sloping down into the coulee, he picked up fresh markings left by a shod horse as well as deer and cattle tracks.

"Hey, Ike!" he shouted. His voice carried up to the top of the coulee to be carried away by the gusting wind.

After Johnny had determined that Walton wasn't in the coulee, he rode out of it to a height where he picked up tracks left by Walton's horse, and he followed them at a walk. They brought Johnny along a ridge; but beyond the ground was composed of hard-packed scoria, and the tracks simply disappeared. Pulling up, he gazed down into a deep draw cut by a creek and another just beyond that, and still another. A gust of wind dashed some loose sand at his face, and he blinked sand out of his left eye as over him came a sensation of loneliness, the feeling that something had happened to Ike Walton. He waited there, searching through those draws for any sign of movement, and after a while a mule deer came nibbling out of some brush. Then he knew his only option was to search the closest draw and work his way northward.

Around five by the sun Johnny rode into camp spread along Big Beaver Creek. They were still branding calfs and mavericks, with Johnny's passage watched silently by other cowhands as he moved toward Bill Lowman and Jake Murdock setting their horses together as Lowman took the tally.

"No sign of him?"

"Nossir. Ike . . . just . . . disappeared . . . ."

"Strange," the rancher said worriedly. "There are some boggy places out there . . . some quicksand."

"I tracked through most of them draws, Mr. Murdock. Figured if Ike got throwed his horse would probably come in with the cattle."

"Well," said Lowman, "his horse didn't." He stared at the sun just touching upon the western buttes. "It'll be dark soon. Walton could come riding in any minute, or not a-tall. And tomorrow for certain we'll see that Yellowstone bunch. They could have found Ike, too, Johnny, or his horse."

"Come on, Johnny," said Jake Murdock. "I'll see that the cook gives you some vittles." The rancher shared a worried look with his segundo before riding toward the chuckwagon with Crowheart.

Worrying over Walton kept Johnny from enjoying the plate of roasted venison and beans. Hannagan, the cook, hearing the gist of what had happened from Jake Murdock, refrained from any small talk as he and the other cook, Jingles, went about the business of preparing the evening meal. There was still plenty

162

of light out when Johnny mounted his bronc and rode over to help watch the day herd beginning to settle in for the night. Some of the cowhands, when circling the herd or waving their ropes to drive back those cattle wanting to graze farther out, stopped for brief chats with Johnny, since they had also learned of Ike Walton's disappearance. Tomorrow morning, rancher Murdock had told Johnny, they would go out looking for Ike Walton. This brought to surface in Crowheart's mind the death of waddy Jamison in that boggy land along Squaw Creek. Something told him that this wasn't the case now, and then some cowhands who were watching cattle farther to the southwest along the Big Beaver flood plain shouted as they spotted a rider coming in at a gallop.

"Doggone, it's Ike!" yelled Johnny as he broke away from the herd and jogged to meet the incoming rider still some distance away. Angling to ride with him were O'Connor and Murdock.

"Riding kind of funny?"

"Maybe he's hurt."

Then, in the collecting darkness, Johnny noticed, too, how Walton's arms were flapping about and that the waddy rode stiffly and so upright that from this distance it appeared he was propped up in the saddle. But he'd recognized that bay of Walton's. They lost sight of the horse pounding down into a low spot, but then it reappeared on a rise and with just enough light remaining to reveal the bloodstained and skinned remains of Ike Walton being fetched toward the cattle by the frenzied bay, its eyes rolled back to show its fear and foam gushing from its flaring nostrils.

Realizing the danger to the herd, Bucky O'Connor

spurred away first, and shouted, "Stop that horse!"

But the cattle were already breaking back toward other cattle being branded, a great surge of over five thousand head trying to get away from the stench of death. Other waddies shouted a warning, the branding crew just managing to make it to the creek but the branding corral being dashed to pieces. The Sibley tent went next, but the wagons still offered stubborn resistance to the cattle flowing around them and those cowhands trying to turn the stampeding cattle. Amongst the cattle went Ike Walton on his bay, bringing sudden fear to the waddies who saw him for the first time. The running cattle had no choice but to crowd the creek as the flood plain narrowed to the northeast, and this slowed them down some. Though the cowhands managed to turn part of the stampede, a lot of cattle broke through and pounded to the northeast along Big Beaver.

In the dust cloud raised by the stampeding cattle, Johnny lost track of where he was or of how long he'd been trying with the others to get the herd under control. Only the moon coming out full kept those chasing the cattle from going under. Since running wasn't the natural gait of cattle, and they were leaned from the long winter, most of them began tiring and slowed down. They scattered into small bunches, and then the stampede was over, with the cattle settling in where they were as if nothing had happened. There were casualties, Johnny was to learn, a 777 hand having his leg shattered and a couple going down, one of them trampled. Back at the camp, a yellow rain slicker had been placed over the body of Jingles the cook. In the glare of the fire started by Woody Hannagan, the eyes of Bill Lowman found Crowheart's.

His voice trembling some, Lowman said. "The same thing happened to Ripley down at Medora. It's got to be the same man done this to Ike Walton."

"Yakima . . . he killed Walton. Over in Miles City him and Yakima Pierce had a disagreement over a poker game. I just happened to be there, me and Ike, down at that bar in Medora when Yakima walked in. One thing led to another. Bill, it's my fault this happened . . . I—"

"Johnny, we're dealing with a crazy man."

It was only then did Crowheart notice the ranchers clustered around in the darkness and staring at him through wondering eyes. They didn't have to say anything, but he knew in a way they blamed him for what had just happened.

A cowhand rode up and said from his saddle, "Carter of the Ox Spread went down; they're bringing the body in now. And another waddy got his leg broken."

"Did they find Walton?"

"Out there someplace. His horse must'a gone down."

Now, beyond the cluster of ranchers and the waddy astride his horse, Johnny suddenly realized Darin Murdock had been there all this time, and in the kid's eyes just before he turned away, Johnny could see a strange unfocused look like a man not concerned over the stampede but angered by it. At that moment Crowheart knew Jake Murdock's son had thrown in with Yakima Pierce and those outlaws. At some curt words from Bill Lowman, Johnny followed the man to their horses.

Lowman said bitterly, "We'll have the others look for Walton's body. Another day and roundup would have been over. Now it'll take us some time to get the cattle together again. And, Johnny, what happened tonight isn't your fault."

"Some of the ranchers think differently." They rode northeasterly along the flood plain.

"Once it sinks in that what happened was just pure craziness on Yakima Pierce's part, they'll come around. It beats me why he was lurking around these parts just waiting to take out Walton."

"Maybe . . . maybe Yakima's part of an outlaw gang."

"Doesn't make sense, men wanting to rustle cattle causin' this stampede. No, we're dealin' with a tetched man in Yakima Pierce. I was you, Crowheart, I'd ride mighty careful from now on."

"Look, Bill, maybe it'd be best you just up and firing me. If only . . . if only I hadn't been in that bar. . . ."

"Lightning don't care who it strikes either, Johnny. Firing you won't prove nothing. You're a good hand. It's Darin I'm worried about."

"Hey!" The shout of a cowhand came farther along the flood plain, and Bill Lowman and Crowheart rode that way, cutting off what Crowheart wanted to tell the segundo about Jake Murdock's son.

Long before sunup the men of the Little Missouri roundup had shucked their bedrolls in favor of their saddled horses as they began the difficult process of regathering the herd. The rising sun revealed a couple of cowhands digging three graves on the bluffs above Big Beaver. Below it showed the wreckage left by the stampeding cattle being held there for the day, or as many days as it would take to find all the cattle. The five ranchers had lingered behind with those watching the herd and the branding crew, and when one of those who'd been using a shovel atop the bluff waved his hat, they began walking three horses bearing the bodies of those who'd been killed up along a game trail. A shout from the skeleton crew watching the day herd held the others there as three riders came loping in from the west along the creek. Jake Murdock commented, "Seems those Yellowstone boys have finished their roundup."

The riders drew up and stared at the bodies wrapped in rain slickers. Their spokesman, Dennison of the W Bar out of Wibaux, said softly, "Sorry to see this, Jake. Happen last night?"

"That it did. Murder's been done—to Walton, one of my hands. But now it's burying time."

"We'll pay our respects." Dismounting and ground-hitching their horses, the newcomers trudged up the game trail behind those going to bury their comrades who suffered needless deaths.

Chapter Thirteen

It remained hot during the long summer, the constant wind helping to dry out the creeks and the Little Missouri holding only a trickle of river water. When it did rain, it came from scattered clouds soon dispersed by the continued heat, and what rainwater that did chance to fall upon the parched Badlands dried up within hours.

This summer also saw the herds of Badlands ranchers being thinned out by outlaw gangs. Cowhands out guarding scattered herds had gone down as had some outlaws. The owner of the Elkhorn Ranch had called an emergency meeting of the Badlands Stockmen's Association, with a telegram sent off requesting that a U.S. marshal be assigned to Billings County, and if that didn't bring results, the next step was to form a vigilante committee.

Profiting from the rustling was Turk Widen and his outlaw gang still using Ezra Morgan's homestead as a jumping-off point whenever they struck a ranch. Widen's lusting after Carrie Morgan had brought a deep resentment from her father, but he would allow the outlaws to stick around as long as money came from Turk Widen on a regular basis. To avoid the longer route down to Medora and the suspicions of any cowpunchers he would encounter along the way, Ezra Morgan bought supplies eastward at Grassy Butte, his other trips up to Watford City. Also of concern to the sodbuster turned wolfer were the signs he'd noticed that an early winter would be settling in, for as July burned into early August a few leaves had turned and birds were gathering. His plans were to leave before snowfall, letting his sons shift for themselves and taking his daughter, Carrie, along to that Oregon country.

For almost a week the outlaws and his sons had been away, and he supposed, from all the loose talk he'd overheard, waiting up at their camp along the Missouri River. Even the wolfer had to admit that Turk Widen had worked out a slick plan, having the other outlaw gangs sell him any cattle they'd rustled, and dirt cheap, then having those Metis pay through the nose for herds. Widen was slick alright, but if the man was so all-fired smart, Morgan thought bitterly as he went about mending one of his traps, why had Widen spent time in that territorial prison? He swung his eyes upon his daughter, who was going out in the heat of late afternoon to tend a garden watered by a natural spring, since the creek had long ago dried up and its twisting bottom lay in baked jumbo clumps that had cracked apart.

Using a hoe to dig weeds away from some beans about ready to be picked, Carrie Morgan had also been thinking of Turk Widen, but in a contemptible way. Her greatest fear was of that big one, Yakima Pierce, a man so filthy of clothing and manner she cringed whenever he was around. She had overheard her brother, Trace, bragging of Yakima's handiwork with a knife on a Hashknife cowpuncher, and it had sickened her, making her realize that only the presence of their father kept her brothers from letting Widen or those other outlaws have their way with her. But uppermost in her mind had been Johnny Crowheart. He was, to her, the shining promise of a future that held love, maybe a place of their own. He hadn't been around these last two months, and since her father would only chase him away, she could understand this long absence. But that she loved Johnny Crowheart there was no doubt. Once in a while his name had come up in the conversation of the outlaws, with Yakima Pierce saying that he would kill Johnny next. Her brother, Joe Bob, had also expressed a desire to confront the man she loved with a sixgun.

"Carrie," called out Ezra Morgan in a rasping voice, "get some vittles to a-warming. And, daughter, fetch me a bottle of whiskey first."

She set the hoe leaning against a tree and went up to the house, and upon bringing a bottle of whiskey out to her father seated in the shade of a run-down shed, she asked, "Think they'll be back tonight?"

"Don't fret about them. Just fix somethin' for the pair of us. That Widen been a-botherin' you again?"

"He's . . . he's hard to keep away from," she said vaguely.

"Well, won't be long a-fore we'll be pullin' out for Oregon. But don't you tell them outlaws or your brothers about this. 'Cause one day when they ride back here we'll be long gone. Now, see to them vittles."

South of Caprock Coulee, and on the northwest corner of land belonging to the Hashknife, the son of Jake Murdock was conferring with Turk Widen, as the other outlaws clustered under cedar trees swaying in the steady wind. They were passing a whiskey bottle around, and George Ramshorn's talk of starting a poker game to while away the time was met with a warning glance from Mack Blackthorn. The Morgan brothers were there, too, full-fledged outlaws now. But none of these men talked about or even missed Kelly Bartow, who was gunned down by a cowpuncher.

"A vigilante committee?"

"That's what's in the wind if a U.S. marshal isn't sent here," said Darin Murdock, enjoying himself and the whiskey he was sharing in.

"We've made a bundle," Widen said dryly. And they had, more money than the outlaw had thought possible. Sooner or later, he realized, the men he rode the outlaw trail with were going to cut loose, head for places where there were plenty of women and liquor and gambling. But those still with him, Blackthorn and Ramshorn, and even Yakima, would keep quiet about all the rustling they'd done. The Morgans were chatterboxes, especially that Joe Bob, always bragging as to how he was gonna blow away that Johnny Crowheart once he came across him. Sad as it seemed, and despite their holding firm when they were out rustling, he had decided that in a little while it would be twilight time for Joe Bob, Abe and Trace. The thought cheered Widen somewhat, as did the idea festering in his mind of killing that old wolfer, Ezra, and having his sport with the man's daughter. She was a bundle, but it troubled him somewhat that Yakima Pierce had also been eying Carrie Morgan. He didn't want to go knife on knife with that buffer hunter under any conditions; that left a sixgun show-down, or just a slug in the back of Yakima's head. First, though, there was this herd of cattle Darin Murdock had been pointing out on a map he'd drawn. The kid had been narrating as to how Jake Murdock was collecting a lot of cattle and would be heading them out in the not too distant future.

"Tell me, kid, don't you have any pangs a-tall about doing your father and them other ranchers thisaway?"

"Do you?" said Darin Murdock.

Shaking his head, the outlaw said, "You are a cold-blooded sonofagun. Kid, if I was to teach you the rudiments of using a handgun"—Widen patted the butt of his—"no telling how many men you'd gun down. And just for the spite of it. You sure that's Crowheart's pocket knife?"

"Here, his initials are carved into the handle. Hey, Trace, pass that bottle over here." He caught the bottle and winked back at Trace Morgan, thinking of all that money he'd salted away. Once his father went bankrupt, Darin Murdock planned to pull out.

"You ever wonder, kid, why I wanted this knife?"

"You told me you were gonna kill a Hashknife

waddy and leave that knife on the body so the others would think Crowheart did it. This time it'll be different, Turk. My dear old daddy'll be with the herd. I'll give five hundred to the man who guns him down."

"You funning us, Murdock?" said Joe Bob Morgan.

"Kill him, Joe Bob, and the money's yours."

Turk Widen grinned around cigarillo smoke spilling away from his face. From the look on the kid's face, he knew it had been a bona fide offer, and if he didn't have so much of his own money stashed away, the gunslinger would have made a go for that five hundred. In a way, the kid was like Yakima Pierce, both having dark moods and wanting blood spilled. During the summer, those times Darin Murdock had come up to Caprock Coulee to collect his share of the rustling money, the kid had seemed more interested in having the Morgan brothers or George Ramshorn tell him who had gone under, or how it felt to kill a man. If the kid wanted blood spilled, why didn't he kill his own pa and save that five hundred dollars. Or perhaps, as Widen suspected, the kid was just building up to killing someone. And afterward, the feel of it in him, there was certain to be a heap of others dying at Darin Murdock's hand. Widen prided himself on his reputation as a gunfighter, but a person like the kid here, or even Yakima for that matter, just wanted to see that pleading look in a man's eyes before his knife or gun put the spark of life out of him. So Turk Widen took a perverse pleasure in what was to come, and right about now.

"Why did I want Crowheart's knife?" he asked

Darin Murdock.

"Yeah?" he responded around a wondering smile.

"To plant as evidence in your body!" Turk Widen smiled when he said that, and it still hadn't registered in Darin Murdock's eyes until Yakima Pierce closing in from behind pulled the gun out of the kid's holster and just stood there waiting for a signal from Widen.

"You . . . you're going to kill me? Why? There's still . . . still a lot of cattle to rustle. It's me, Turk, who set this thing up."

"Kid, the honeymoon's over."

Even as Darin Murdock turned to make a break for his horse, the heavy left hand of Yakima Pierce came clubbing at his head to knock him against a tree. He grunted in pain and raised a feeble arm to ward off Yakima's next blow, only to have blood and teeth come spilling out of his mouth, and he sagged to the ground.

"Here," said Turk Widen, as he tossed Crowheart's pocket knife to the buffalo hunter. "We'll be at Ezra's." He had little stomach for what was to come, as did his men. But what Trace Morgan said next surprised the outlaws and his brothers.

"Think I'll wait for Yakima."

Joe Bob Morgan, as he swung aboard his horse, said, "Trace, I knew you was always a little different from me and Abe, and Pa . . . but, Trace, you sure about this?"

"Yakima's my friend. Gonna teach me his ways. Ain't that right, Yakima?"

The buffalo hunter merely grunted as he set about tying Darin Murdock's wrists together with a length of rope, then throwing the rope over a convenient branch, raising the unconscious man up to leave him dangling. His mind set for what was to come, the need to bring pain to one of his own kind strong in Yakima Pierce's mind. Somehow, he would suffer with Darin Murdock, as he had suffered with all of them buffalo he done in and skinned. Though he resented the presence of Trace Morgan, Yakima made no comment as he splashed water over Jake Murdock's son to awaken him for the ritual of what was to come.

But Turk Widen had something to say, his words reaching those riding with him before they were flung away by the wind.

"Three crazies getting together to play some pinochle."

The outlaws, spurring their horses into the collecting darkness, never looked back again.

The sound of their horses neighing caused one of the two Hashknife waddies sharing a line shack to reach for a rifle and handgun, while the other doused the coal oil lamp.

The second waddy muttered, "Sounds like our horses want to break out of that corral."

The other cowpoke glanced out a window and tried to get the lay of what had disturbed their horses. Then he eased over and cracked open the only door. "Don't see nothing."

But what he saw next as he opened the door wider made him double over wretching. Gasping, he blun-

176

dered out the door, followed by his partner, with the two waddies only able to stand there and stare helplessly at the horse that had just arrived. They finally came forward, one of them grabbing the reins as the horse reared in an attempt to dislodge its saddle and the object tied to it. Blood seemed to be everywhere, staining the saddle and the withers and shoulders of the terrified horse, the stench entering the nostrils of the waddies. In the corral their horses were cluttered at its opposite side and snorting their fear.

"Fetch the lantern!" said Arty Lamar as he tied the reins to a corral pole and then stepped back, the barrel of the rifle he held dropping to point at the barren ground. "And . . . and a knife to cut them ropes!"

The other cowpuncher came out again bearing the lighted lantern and a knife, and he closed warily on the horse while holding the lantern up to see if he knew the dead man lashed to the saddle and held upright with the help of crossed branches lashed together. The face hadn't been marked, but the torso was an open wound.

Lamar exclaimed disbelievingly, "It's Murdock's son! It's Darin Murdock!" Sunken hilt deep into the chest was a knife.

"Get some blankets or tarp while I cut him off that horse. Do it now."

"I can't believe it, Arty, can't believe it's Darin."

"It's him alright. First all this rustling — now this. We'll get him down. Then wrap him in something. Then saddle up and take him back to the ranch."

"Tonight?"

"We won't be getting any sleep anyway . . . not

177

after this."

The outlaws clattering in roused Ezra Morgan and his daughter, the wolfer going for his rifle. He eased out the side door and made certain it was his sons skylined by moonlight before he shouted for Carrie to light a lantern.

As he dismounted, Mack Blackthorn said quietly to Widen, "That Murdock kid didn't deserve to be turned over to Yakima. Maybe he could still have helped us out."

"So, Mack, you're asking why I had him killed? He had no qualms about putting up five hundred to see his pa gunned down. I had this feeling he was getting ready to cut and run. But run where? Miles City? Down to Deadwood? Wherever it was, Mack, he would have turned us in."

"Who would believe a lying kid like that, anyway?"

"You and me, and Ramshorn, have got paper out on us from here to Hades and back. Who would believe him? Any lawman would just love to collect all that reward money out on us. Dead men don't talk."

"You mentioned taking care of the Morgans, too—"

"Not until we get them cattle of Jake Murdock's and bring them up along the Missouri. That'll be another . . . say around ten thousand, them Metis will pay us." He turned and called out to Joe Bob Morgan just turning his unsaddled horse loose in the corral. "Say, Joe Bob, how's about hustling over to the house and telling your sister to get some chow to warming."

"Abe's done looking into that. Got some more whiskey stashed in the barn in case you gents is interested."

Around a smile Turk Widen said, "Just trot that white lightning out, old buddy."

Inside the sod house, Abe Morgan dropped his hat on an unvarnished chair as he told how Widen had outwitted young Darin Murdock. "That Murdock kid sure thought he had this all figured out, Pa. Even wanted to pay someone to kill his own pa. That's cruel, that is. But old Turk Widen made sure they'd pin the killing on that cowpoke . . . Crowheart. First of all, Pa, he, Turk that is, had young Murdock steal this waddy's pocket knife; got his initials on it and all. So when they find it on Murdock's body . . ." He grinned and slapped an appreciative hand down at his hip.

"Cold-blooded killing, Abe, is not to be taken lightly. Where's Trace?"

"Why, Pa, Trace is helping Yakima out."

Ezra Morgan came off the chair as he picked up his rifle, and he shouted, "You left your brother with that bloodthirsty buffalo hunter?"

"Shucks, Pa, Trace wanted to stay."

"You know your brother ain't all that smart in the head. And neither are you, for that matter." Now some of the bluster left the wolfer as Widen came in trailed by the others, with all of them settling down in the small living room. Right away, he noticed bitterly, the gaze of the outlaw leader swung through the kitchen door to fasten upon Carrie Morgan standing

179

by the stove. "Widen, I got a message for you."

"Let's hear it, Ezra."

"The Drago gang is holding around four hundred head of cattle up at Wild Cow Bay. They don't hear from you before the week's out, they'll drive that herd across the border."

"That's easy pickings," said Mack Blackthorn. "Should be no trouble driving that herd over to our camp."

"Okay, we'll head up there soon's Trace and Yakima get back."

"I'm worried about this U.S. marshal coming in."

Widen swung his lusting gaze from Carrie Morgan to her brother, Joe Bob. "One man can't stop all the rustling. Too many gangs working the Badlands. Boys, I don't ever want to get off this gravy train."

In the kitchen, Carrie Morgan moved so they couldn't see her from the living room. She couldn't believe her brothers helping to frame Johnny Crowheart. They had changed since coming here, or had they always been this way, and she'd simply overlooked a lot of their faults. When her mother had run away, Carrie was going on twelve, and too young to understand why her father had thrown the family bible away, vowing never to set foot in a church again. That he would take money from these outlaws troubled Carrie more than she had cared to admit. Now it was blood money, with both her father and brothers sharing in the death of Darin Murdock, along with others they had killed this summer during their rustling forays. And what about Johnny? Harm would surely come to him once they determined he'd committed murder. Now she could feel any love that remained in her for her family slipping away. They were no better than Turk Widen, or that buffalo hunter, Yakima Pierce. Somehow she must warn Johnny Crowheart, even tell him she'd run away with him and damn what happened to the Morgan clan.

"Daughter, how're them vittles coming?"

"Just about done, Pa."

Chapter Fourteen

Someone hammering on the back door of his log house brought Bill Lowman out of the bed and shouting worriedly, "Okay, I hear you!" His chief concern was that rustlers had hit again. A groping hand found the Levis, and he slipped into them and his boots, as his eyes adjusted to middle-of-the-night darkness. Hurrying into the kitchen, he opened the door and stared quizzingly at Arty Lamar.

"It's Jake's son—done in the same as Ike Walton."

He moved ahead of Lamar over to a horse packing the body of Darin Murdock wrapped in a tarp, and the segundo said roughly, "Get him off that horse." He swung to face Lamar as the other hand, Si Reese, lowered the body to the ground.

"Darin's horse just came wandering in. It was inhuman, Bill, the kid being tied upright in the saddle and all cut up like that. I'll have nightmares about this for a long time."

Nodding, Lowman went over and crouched down, pulling the tarp away to expose Darin Murdock's face, which to his surprise hadn't been sliced up though it was puffy from having the eyes gouged out. He felt sick to his stomach, angry and plain bewildered. Now

Darin, he thought sadly, wouldn't have to go around hating his father anymore, or anyone else.

"Here's the murder weapon—took it out of his chest."

Coming erect, he cast puzzled eyes upon the pocket knife Lamar had just handed him. It was no accident that horse coming into Lamar's line camp. Whoever killed Darin wanted the body found and identified. But he doubted the pocket knife was the murder weapon, this after pulling out the blade and running his thumb along the dull edge. A skinning job like this required a bigger knife, one so sharp a man could shave with it.

"That's Crowheart's knife!"

"Johnny's?"

"Seen him using it when we rode together. Johnny's initials are carved into the handle."

Turning the knife over, he could see by moonlight two letters: J. C. Yesterday morning he'd asked two of the waddies bunking here at the home place if they wanted to bodyguard Felipe Lopez while he went to Medora for supplies. Crowheart begged off. He hadn't pushed it. But the fact remained Crowheart had been in that town when that 777 cowpoke had been murdered. Was it just coincidence him being partnered up with Ike Walton during spring roundup, and the last man to see Walton alive. After suppering tonight, Crowheart had gone for a ride; there was nothing unusual about that. Maybe he had rendezvoused with Carrie Morgan. Or, and somehow this didn't fit Johnny's character, he had gone out and killed Jake's son. Now for the ranch foreman came the truly hard part, telling the man he worked for that his son was dead.

A deep sadness welled up in Bill Lowman as he said, "Put the boy's body in my house." He was not only thinking of Jake Murdock, but of Rose Lopez, a kindly woman who had raised Darin after his mother had run away. With that bad heart of hers, something of this nature could see her suffering a heart attack. All of a sudden Bill Lowman felt old, too, sort of washed out, and then he began that long and painful walk over to the main house. The glow of a lamp surprised him as Felipe Lopez opened the back porch door.

"I heard them riding in, Señor Bill. There is trouble?"

"The worst kind. Would you go and roust Jake."

"I'm getting up." Jake Murdock's voice came distantly from inside the house, and then he appeared, pulling his suspenders over his shoulders and moving out onto the back porch. "A horse coming in this time of night always did break my sleep; hard to break old habits, I reckon. Well, Bill, is it rustlers again?"

"Jake, it's your son."

"He's dead isn't he?"

"Arty Lamar and Reese brought him in. I . . . I had them put Darin over in my shack, Jake."

"There's more to this than him getting thrown by a horse, isn't there?"

Reluctantly, and painfully, Lowman said, "There is." The pocket knife felt heavy in his hand, and for some reason he didn't want to show it to the owner of the Hashknife; but it was something that had to be done. "He was murdered, Jake. The same as Walton . . . and that 777 waddy down at Medora. And this —

he held up the knife — "was stuck in your boy's chest. The knife belongs to Johnny Crowheart."

"To . . . Crowheart? He killed my boy?"

"That I don't know," said Lowman. "But I have to tell you that Crowheart went for a ride tonight. Came back around ten-thirty, eleven. But that wouldn't give him enough time to get up to that line camp and back. There's got to be others involved in this."

"Reckon we won't know who until we talk to Crowheart," Murdock said grimly as he swung around and pulled a Winchester off a gun rack, then levered a shell into its breech.

"Jake, don't you want to see your son first? We don't know it was Johnny Crowheart who did this. And if you kill him, we might never find out who these others are."

"Dammit, Bill, my son's dead . . . murdered—"

Lowman turned as the waddies who'd brought in the body came up to the house, and then he stepped forward and held out his hand. "We'll go and get Crowheart. Please, Jake, I'll take that rifle."

The rancher sighed deeply and closed his eyes to hide how he felt from the others, and the Lowman pulled the rifle from his hands. Motioning to the waddies, Bill Lowman led them toward the bunkhouse. When they got there, he said quietly, "Arty, take Si with you and watch the back door."

"Sure you can handle this?"

"My job," he said simply.

Wordlessly he moved to the front door of the long, low building and eased inside. He had little difficulty finding Crowheart's bunk, since most of the waddies were out at line camps tending to the cattle, a handful doing chores and watching the cattle grazing nearby. Stepping up to the bunk, it struck him that Crowheart wasn't having any trouble sleeping just after killing a man. Or maybe he'd misjudged the young waddy. Crowheart's gunbelt hung from a wall peg; his rifle was below that leaning against the wall.

Reaching out, he shook Crowheart's shoulder. "Johnny, get up."

"Yeah . . . yeah . . . that you, Bill?"

Lowman took a wooden match out of a shirt pocket and used it to light one of the lamps, all the while letting his gaze slide to Crowheart, who was trying to figure out this reason for being woken up.

Crowheart finally said, "Those rustlers strike again?"

"Nope," said Lowman. "Johnny, is this your knife?"

"Why" — he grinned — "where'd you find that. Sure it is. Lost it a couple of days ago."

"We found it . . . in Darin's body. . . ."

Shock widened Johnny Crowheart's eyes, and the segundo curled a finger around the trigger of his Winchester just in case the waddy made a play for his gun. But all Crowheart did was stare at the knife as he tried to make sense out of the segundo's words, and then he asked, "How? I just saw Darin this morning. Heading out someplace, I think."

"He died the same as Walton."

"Skinned like that?" Some of the color left Johnny's face. "I knew he was mixed up in something . . . but, getting done in this way."

"What do you mean he was involved in something?"

"All I know, Bill, is that I saw him drinking with the Morgan brothers and some outlaws in a Little Misery saloon."

"You should have told me this," he said accusingly.

"Tried to, a couple of times. Guess I didn't want to hurt Mr. Murdock."

"He's hurt a-plenty now. Afraid I'm gonna have to tie you up, Johnny."

"Wait a minute, Bill. I didn't kill Jake's son!"

"You, and you," Lowman said to a couple of hands, along with four others who'd gotten up, "get some rope." Then he turned to Crowheart, "Sorry, but I've got no choice."

"I told you, Bill, I lost my knife. Maybe here in the bunkhouse . . . or around the buildings. But I didn't kill Darin Murdock." He stood up and gazed blankly at the other cowhands, and back at Bill Lowman. "It could have been one of the Morgans doing this, or Yakima Pierce."

"That old buffalo hunter?"

"Remember, me and Walton had that run-in with Yakima down at Medora, the day I hired on here."

"Hard to forget something like that." Lowman swung his gaze to the waddies returning with short lengths of rope. "I want to believe you, Johnny, but this knife is pretty hard evidence. Tomorrow we'll take you over to Dickinson. Suppose you'll have to stand trial."

"But, Bill, doggonit, I'm . . . innocent. . . ."

First light carried Jake Murdock away from the main house at a purposeful walk. He carried a bullwhip, a rope on which he's fastened a hangman's noose, and this terrible anger. This talk of his segundo's of taking Crowheart over to Dickinson to be jailed had torn at Jake Murdock. There, some smooth-talking gent with a law degree would con a jury into letting the waddy go. At the moment the rancher was blinded to his son's faults. All he knew was that his only kin had been murdered. Now he would have his revenge, for his son, and Ike Walton, and mostly for the Hashknife.

This wasn't like spring roundup when the men were rousted at three, and most of them were just stirring, dressing or smoothing out the blankets on their bunks. Arty Lamar, peering into a shard of mirror as he shaved, saw the door open first and then what the rancher had brought with him. He stopped shaving in a hurry. Si Reese and the four remaining hands stared anxiously at the man they worked for as he went up and gazed down at Crowheart, looked back from where he lay thonged on his bunk.

Dropping the coiled rope on an empty bunk, Jake Murdock unlimbered the bullwhip. His rage was too strong to express with words, and sweeping the bullwhip back, he lashed out at the waddy. Crowheart shuddered under the impact of the leather thong tearing at his flesh, and somehow he managed to gasp the pain away. This time the thick leather whip struck him in the upper chest, tearing the heavy shirt he had on and leaving a welt. He struggled off the bunk to get away from that whip and landed on his side, with Murdock coming at him again. The whip snaked around his arm, and when Jake Murdock snapped it back, bits of flesh came with it. Now an agonized scream poured out of Johnny Crowheart.

"No! I didn't kill your son! Please . . . I swear

189

it. . . ."

"I trusted you, damn you!" As the rancher struck again, one of the hands slipped out the back door and ran toward Bill Lowman's log house. Breathing heavily, Murdock lowered the whip to his side and stared at the shredded clothing clinging to the cowpoke's body. Tossing the whip away, he stepped over and picked up the rope he'd brought along. "You, Lamar, get a horse and bring it over to that big oak by the blacksmith shop."

Johnny was dimly aware of the rancher slipping the noose around his neck and tightening it so that he could barely draw air into his heaving lungs, but he was horribly aware of the pain coming from his lacerated body. Now Jake Murdock brought the rope down and looped it around Crowheart's ankles. Straightening up, he slipped the end he held over his shoulder and began dragging Crowheart toward the front door. Then Bill Lowman came into the bunkhouse.

"Jake? I can't believe this."

"Reese, cover him."

Si Reese unleathered his handgun and looked anxiously at the segundo as though he didn't want to get involved in this, and Lowman said, "No need for that, Jake. Maybe it's true like Crowheart said, that someone stole his knife. Look at him, Jake, all cut to ribbons."

"Not as bad as my son got it," said Murdock. "Stand aside or so help me I'll kill you myself!"

Lowman stepped away from the door, and after the rancher had dragged Johnny Crowheart over the sill and down the steps, he went outside, too, angry that he had backed down. This whole affair had a bad stench to it. Then he saw Arty Lamar leading an unsaddled horse toward the blacksmith shop and knew that they were going to hang Crowheart. Turning, he saw that Si Reese had forgotten about him and was following after Murdock. He came at the waddy low and at an angle, grabbed the man's shoulder to spin him, and struck Si Reese along the jawbone. As the man went down, Lowman retrieved the Navy Colt and started after Jake Murdock, who was just hoisting Crowheart onto the horse held steady by Lamar. He got there just as Murdock had thrown the rope over a thick oaken branch.

Only he didn't have to use the gun or say a word, for loping around the house were three men he'd never seen before, and with them, the editor of the Badlands Cowboy, Arthur Packard. There was no mistaking the U.S. marshal's badge pinned to the chest of a lanky man astride a blooded horse.

"I'm Con Tillison—U.S. marshal out of Billings. Which one of you is Murdock?"

"That's me," the rancher said testily. "And you're way off your reservation, Tillison."

"Do you have an explanation as to why you're hanging this man?"

"He murdered my son!"

"He appears to be half-dead himself. Gowdy, get him off that horse."

"No, he's to hang!" As the rancher brought his weight to bear on the rope and lifted Johnny up from the horse, the gun in Bill Lowman's hand barked. The rope parted with a dull twang, and Crowheart fell heavily to the ground as the horse broke away.

Easing his half-drawn Peacemaker back into its

holster, Marshal Tillison threw the segundo an appreciative smile. The upper lip mustache was thick and shaggy, and like the two deputy marshals, Con Tillison was all sinew and bone and sun-baked flesh. He looked to be in his forties, but had just turned thirty-one; his was a demanding profession.

"Mr. Murdock," said Tillison, "I didn't mean to spoil your fun. As for why I'm here, your stockmen's association is responsible for that. You know Mr. Packard. And you are . . ."

"Segundo out here; Bill Lowman. I'll leave you to talk with Jake. Best tend to Crowheart." When he looked at the rancher, the man evaded his eyes, and somehow Lowman knew that his actions of a moment ago in defending Crowheart had just broken a long friendship. Cradling the young waddy in his arms, Lowman went toward his house to leave the story of how this had happened to the bossman of the Hashknife.

At first he hadn't been sure, and now Bill Lowman knew it was a woman riding that grey southward along Squaw Creek. He'd brought his bronc into a clump of willows, the sun dimmed most of the day by sullen grey clouds. Ever since they'd buried Darin Murdock, going on a week now, the weather had been getting colder. Maybe his death had provoked a weather change. In any case, Johnny Crowheart had been taken by Marshal Tillison down to Medora. A territorial judge would be coming in every so often, the marshal had told them, and back there right now was a man intimately familiar with the workings of a gallows.

The Hashknife waddies were busy culling out the cattle that would be sent to fall market. As a rule, Jake Murdock would be out there every day, but since his son had died, the rancher had gone into a shell, rarely leaving the house, and issuing orders to his segundo through Felipe Lopez. To tell the truth, Lowman expected to be given his walking papers, since Jake never like to be bucked at anything. It would have been a mistake to hang Johnny Crowheart, and maybe Jake realized that now; but he would never admit this to Lowman or anyone else.

When a snowflake curled down and brushed against his cheek, Lowman looked upward in surprise. He always did like that first snowfall, but not this unseasonably early, and it worried him. Too many cattle had over-grazed the grasslands, both in the Badlands and westward. A long winter would kill a lot of cattle—one with heavy snow could prove disastrous. And even though he didn't own any cattle, Bill Lowman wouldn't be anything else than a cattleman. A month ago he's gone to town to see that Jo Ann girl, and much to his surprise she'd come up with the notion of him trying for his own ranch. Not at his age, he'd told her.

As if sensing Lowman's presence, Carrie Morgan had pulled up her grey out along the creek, and she was about to whirl her horse around when the segundo showed himself. They eyed one another across a distance of about twenty rods, until he broke the silence.

"I expect you came to see Johnny." Her quiet beauty surprised Lowman, and in a way he envied

Crowheart.

"Are you . . . Lowman?"

"Yup, been him for too many years, Carrie." They brought their horses together, the few lazy flakes swirling around them and the main buildings just beyond that bend in the creek. "Trouble is, Johnny isn't here."

"Did he quit the Hashknife?" Worry showed plain in her eyes.

"U.S. Marshal Con Tillison showed up and arrested Johnny. Jailed him at Medora. Good thing, too, or . . . well, no matter what would have happened."

"Then it's too late to warn him." She turned the collar of her coat up.

"You know something, Miss Morgan. If it would help Johnny, I sure wish you'd tell me."

"What I know, Mr. Lowman, could see my brothers arrested or hung—my pa, too. Would you believe me if I told you Johnny didn't kill Darin Murdock? That it was Darin who stole Johnny's pocket knife?"

"Darin? I don't understand?"

"Turk Widen asked him to steal Johnny's knife. That it was to be left as evidence after they rustled some cattle and killed a cowhand, the idea being to plant the knife on his body."

"Whoa, Carrie, you're going a little too fast for me. Just who is this Turk Widen?"

"He heads up an outlaw gang."

"Would one of them outlaws be a buffer hunter named Yakima Pierce."

"Yes," she said, glancing over her shoulder as if she expected Yakima to be there. "All I know is that Yakima killed Darin Murdock."

194

"What about your brothers, are they—"

"No," she said sharply, "no more. I . . . I can't tell you any more. Just tell Johnny that . . . I love him." Wheeling her horse away, Carrie Morgan spurred it into a gallop while glancing back to see if the segundo would come after her, and when she did, Bill Lowman could see the tears staining her cheeks.

Shoving his hat to the back of his head, he just sat there with his hands folded over the saddle horn, stunned by Carrie Morgan's revelations as to who had killed Darin Murdock. Just what part had Darin Murdock played in all of this? This would explain, pondered Lowman, why Darin had always found some excuse to get away from the ranch, and there were those times he'd been absent during spring roundup. Come to think on it, the ranchers hit hardest by rustlers had been those involved in the Little Missouri roundup. That must be it, Darin Murdock telling that Widen bunch just where these ranchers would be summering their cattle, even how many waddies were keeping watch over these herds.

Grimacing at the light snowfall, Bill Lowman, troubled and damning the son of Jake Murdock for what he'd done, also realized Darin Murdock had signed his own death warrant when he'd hooked up with those outlaws. If they could kill Darin, and if Carrie's brothers were in on this, Lowman would bet his last double eagle that Joe Bob, Trace and Abe didn't have too many breathing days left.

Tomorrow he would ramrod a herd of Hashknife cattle being driven down to Medora, some of them to be railroaded east on Northern Pacific cattle cars, the rest already sold to the Marquis de Mores. When he got there, ranch foreman Bill Lowman meant to have a lot of private words with Johnny Crowheart. He owed Johnny something, for the whipping the young waddy had taken, and for not believing that he was innocent. He owed Carrie Morgan something, too; just keeping Johnny alive until the real killer was brought to justice.

Chapter Fifteen

In a town without law and where lawmen just passed through, a star-packer checking into the Rough Riders Hotel brought a lot of people out into the street. By the way they dressed, and armed like that, two of the men with U.S. Marshal Con Tillison had to be his deputies. The other man got some to thinking he was either a preacher or territorial judge dappered up as he was in a black stovepipe hat, frock coat and matching black trousers.

On the shaded porch fronting his billiard emporium, Genial Jim was willing to lay odds the man was a judge. But a few hardcases among the onlookers knew otherwise, that stowed on the packhorse were the ropes and paraphernalia of a hangman. Hangman Elias Poe paused before following the deputies into the hotel and turned slowly to survey the crowd. He was over six feet, but too thin for his height, and had hands with big wrist bones and penetrating eyes sunk deep into their sockets in a face stretched tight against his skull. That searching look caused a few to go seeking a saloon or their horses. Later that afternoon a trip to a hardware store by Elias Poe brought the story quickly spreading through town that he'd purchased the hardware and lumber needed to build a gallows. And before heading up to the Elkhorn Ranch to palaver with its owner, Teddy Roosevelt, Marshal Con Tillison scouted out a place to use as a temporary jail, which turned out to be one of Genial Jim's storage sheds, whereupon he hired a carpenter to board up its two windows and put a new lock on the door.

By nightfall everyone in Medora, and Little Misery, knew law and order had descended upon Billings County.

About a week later the marshal and his deputies reappeared in Medora with Johnny Crowheart earning the distinction of being their first prisoner. He was still in no shape to ride, and it had been editor Packard who'd talked the marshal into having them take Crowheart over to Doc Henderson's.

"Marshal Tillison, is this any way to treat a prisoner?"

"I had no hand in that whipping." Unruffled by the doctor's put-out attitude, Con Tillison left his deputies there to watch his prisoner and strode with the editor of the Badlands Cowboy in the general direction of the Rough Riders Hotel. A week together had pretty much talked them out. But Packard had a final question.

"I don't see how three men think they can stop this rustling."

"We don't intend doing this by our lonesome."

"Does that mean you've requested a detachment of the U.S. cavalry—"

"Nothing as drastic as that, Mr. Packard."

"Just what can I tell my readers?"

"It's going to be a tough winter. Tougher on them

rustlers."

As the days passed, Johnny Crowheart's body healed, but he knew there'd be some scars, on his arms and upper body, and mentally. Through a chink in one of the windows he oftentimes watched hangman Elias Poe laboring to erect his gallows. Down the street would go an occasional rider or buggy, and the stagecoach always came this way as it headed for the Medora-to-Deadwood office to dislodge its passengers, with townspeople strolling by on the jailward side of street rather than venturing too close to the gallows. There was also his glimpse of the trail winding down from the north on the edge of the bluffs, and of Northern Pacific freight and passenger trains. He was fed twice a day; the meals catered from the Cowboy Cafe and brought by Windom Brown, the part-time town marshal. Brown was a sad-faced man favoring a left hand broken some time back by a bucking bronc. The bones had never been set right, and that left arm crooked in and the hand was withered; but Windom Brown never complained, though he would go on a bender about twice a year. He didn't have a gun belt but a big clumsy Dragoon tucked under his belt. And, now, when he appeared on the street, Crowheart sighed bitterly and stood in traceries of sunlight filtering through the window as he heard the key being turned in the heavy metal lock.

"Supper," Brown muttered indifferently, as with a cautious hand he opened the door and made sure his prisoner was where he should be, back by one of the bunks, before he shuffled over the threshold and deposited the plate and cup he'd brought on a small table. "How you feeling?"

"Better."

"Nights are getting that feel of winter. Sorry about there not being a stove in here."

"I could use some more blankets," Johnny said edgily. "And maybe something to read."

"I'll see to it."

"Has that U.S. marshal got back yet?"

"Nope."

"You got any idea when that judge is gonna show up?"

"I expect, Crowheart, the waiting to see what happens is the worst part. Can't blame you none for feeling that way. That hangman hammering away all day don't help you none either."

"You could just let me walk out that door."

"Expect I could, Crowheart. But I won't. Then it'll be me hopscotching up them gallow's steps. Blankets — I'll rustle some up . . . and fetch you a Police Gazette or something else to read. Got enough oil in that lantern?"

"Getting low, but enough for tonight. And, Windom, I appreciate this."

When the door closed, Johnny sat down at the table and ate slowly, trying to fight back the dread of anticipation over what was to come. The town marshal had brought him the trend of what the townspeople felt about this, the odds being that Johnny Crowheart would have the distinct honor of being the first man hung in Billings County. One day Genial Jim had showed up for a brief visit, but nobody else. And Crowheart had become a very lonely young man.

Deliberately he had kept from thinking about Carrie, telling himself that she would find a better man than him. She was some woman, though — with eyes that melted a man's heart as did that once in a while smile. In her, he felt, was this wanting to get away from her family, for by now she must know her brothers had turned to rustling and murder.

When his jailor returned and swung the door open, to his surprise Johnny gazed at the lazy snowflakes cascading upon the street. Across the way, Elias Poe had quit for the day, and Windom Brown said, "Got these magazines, too. This snow keeps up you'll be needin' some heat in here. Don't see why a stove can't be installed. G'night, Crowheart."

Just as Brown began closing the door, Johnny saw cattle surging in from the north, with cowhands hazing them down into the flats below, and he said around a smile, "Maybe I could hire on with that outfit."

"You get cleared of this murder charge, Crowheart, I reckon so."

The men of the Hashknife felt better when they saw the welcoming lights of Medora and the holding pens strung along the railroad tracks. Coming out to confer with ranch foreman Bill Lowman was a cattle buyer who'd already contracted to buy two thousand head of prime beef. Others swinging out at a canter were the Marquis de Mores and five men working at his meat packing plant, here to help the waddies bring the other fifteen hundred head of cattle over to other pens at the plant.

"Gentlemen," Lowman said to the Marquis and the cattle buyer, "Jake Murdock's regrets that he can't be here."

"Yes," said the Marquis. "After what happened to his son, I can understand. A regretable incident. Mr. Lowman, the cattle are in fine shape. Only the weather seems to be spoiling everything. So, I know you'll want to check into your hotel. We can get together tomorrow — say around ten?"

"Anytime."

"Yes, Mr. Lowman," the cattle buyer agreed. "I'd prefer talking in a nice cozy room myself."

The task of bringing cattle unused to gates or pens into these wooden places of confinement consumed the early hours of the evening, and with the snow coming down heavier, colder, all of the waddies were forced to don sheepskins or rain slickers. But knowing that when the job was finished they could do a little carousing, there was little complaining. And engrossed in the task at hand, no one noticed a solitary rider loping down from the north.

It didn't take Carrie Morgan over a half hour to locate the shack where Crowheart was being held and find out from a local that Town Marshal Windom Brown lived over at the Hotel de Mores. Bringing her horse close to the shack, lantern light poking out through small openings in the boards covering the windows told her the man she loved was awake. She resisted the temptation to call out to him, for to do so could attract attention; and Carrie swung her horse away and brought it at a walk toward a livery stable. Riding behind the building, she left her horse there, then slipped inside and made certain she was alone before picking out a rangy sorrel and saddling the horse. Then, going out the front door, Carrie Morgan hurried through the cold fall night. A passing cowpuncher threw her a curious glance as she went into the lobby of the Hotel de Mores.

The night clerk looked up from his checker board and said, "Yes, can I help you?"

"Marshal Brown, is he in his room?"

"I think he's still there. Why?"

"Oh . . . my husband . . . there's been a fight . . . and—"

"Upstairs," said the night clerk, turning back to his checker board as Carrie bounded up the staircase. Then he shouted at her, "Room 212."

Unbuttoning her coat, Carrie palmed the Navy Colt she'd stolen from her father and stepped to the door and called out, "Marshal Brown, you in there? There's been a fight!"

As the door swung wide, Carrie Morgan brought up the heavy gun with both hands and came at the marshal. "Stand clear, Marshal, or I swear I'll kill you."

"You betcha," he said shakily while stumbling backward and bumping into the dresser. "Easy, missy, that fool thing could go off."

Closing the door, she said, "I want the key to the jail!"

"What about this fight?"

"The key or I'll kill you! Now!"

"Sure," he mumbled, with his face paling as he fumbled a ring of keys out of a coat pocket. At her command to toss it on the bed he did so.

"Now, turn around." And when he did, Carrie

slashed out with the butt of the Navy Colt and hit him on the head. He came down hard onto a chair, then fell from there to the floor. Then she used the marshal's belt and some rope she found in the room to hogtie him along with wadding up a handkerchief and sticking it in his mouth, tying it there with a piece of torn pillowcase. Hooked on a wall peg was a gunbelt which she recognized as Crowheart's, and by the dresser, his rifle. Since the town of Medora had yet to erect a jail, Marshal Windom Brown used this hotel room as a half-hearted office; and tonight it was a windfall for Carrie as it had given her Johnny's guns. Her eyes landed upon a bedroll on a shelf in the only closet and a Mackinaw, both items which she liberated from the closet, and then she stole out of the room and found the back staircase.

Back at the livery stable, she tied the bedroll behind the saddle on the sorrel, then thrust the rifle into the scabbard before leading it out back. She mounted her horse and went cautiously toward where Johnny was being held, the heavy snowfall keeping the streets mostly empty. Reining up in back of the shack, Carrie came around the building by the door. "Johnny, it's me, Carrie!" she said.

"Carrie?" His eyes lifted from the magazine he'd been browsing through. He hopped up from the chair and hurried over to the door. "You're here?"

"Get dressed," she said in a hushed voice but lilting with urgency and a trace of excitement.

"Cold as it is in here I'm wearing all I own." But he went over and wedged his hat over his head, slipping into his sheepskin and putting on his leather gloves. As Carrie unlocked the door, he remembered to douse the lantern.

"Let's go!"

He stepped outside. "Where?"

"First, out of Medora." She closed and locked the door and threw the key away, and then grabbing his arm, she brought the wondering cowpuncher around back and to their horses. "The sorrel's yours."

"Carrie, I . . . I can't believe this . . . that you'd come—"

"I'm here, Crowheart. Now get aboard that cayuse so's we can head out of here."

He did so, gladly, with that surprised look still engraved on his face. She rode at a canter away from the shack to find a cross street, and then continued at the same gait northeasterly, going out the same way she'd come in, but with her man this time.

"Carrie, this'll brand you an outlaw for certain."

"For certain it will, Crowheart. Up north along the Little Missouri there's an abandoned cabin. Before coming in to Medora I scouted it out. Then rustled up some firewood and left my saddlebags there."

"Damn, if you ain't something."

"Johnny Crowheart, I've heard enough of cursing from my kin. I came . . . well, I came because I just happen to love you, you jug-eared galoot. And . . . and I went down and told your foreman, Lowman, about you not killing that rancher's son."

"Gee, Carrie, I don't know what to say. What . . . what did Bill Lowman think? Did he believe you?"

"Here." She lifted his gunbelt from where it had been hooked over her saddle horn and handed it to him, with their eyes reaching out to caress one another. The Mackinaw she'd taken fitted loosely over

205

her own coat, and someday, Carrie was hoping, she could return it. "He believed me, Johnny. More importantly, he knows you didn't kill Darin Murdock. That the killer is Yakima Pierce."

"That helps a whole heap, Carrie."

"Can't you say it, Crowheart?"

"Say what?"

"That you love me—"

Swinging in closer, he said loudly, "I'll love you always." His lips brushed against her cheek, and then Carrie and Johnny brought their horses into a gallop as Medora disappeared in the snowy night.

"Mr. Lowman, what I'm really trying to say is that someone else has asked me to marry him."

Cattleman Bill Lowman lowered his coffee cup where he sat across from Jo Ann Newkirk in one of the booths in the Oyster Grotto. For a moment he couldn't think of anything to say. The sun was up but shining dully through a grey sky, and a few scattered flakes were still coming down. In pairs and by threes some of the other Hashknife cowpokes had come in for breakfast or just for warming coffee. Lowman had been telling her that the murder of Jake's son had changed things out at the Hashknife—that he was considering striking out to Montana and trying something else. She was younger than he—at least ten years, he figured—but a woman who made him feel comfortable whenever he came around. He'd taken her out a few times, to socials around Medora, and once over to the Chateau de Mores to attend one of the many parties held by the Marquis and his lovely wife, Medora. Along a memorable trip on a Northern Pacific passenger train eastward to Dickinson, Jo Ann did some shopping while he attended to some ranch business with Jake Murdock, who'd come along.

"I see," he murmured. "Anyone I know?"

"A rancher, Bill. It's just that I don't love him. But I suppose what he's offering me in the way of security makes up for that."

"I suppose. What you're saying, too, is that old Bill Lowman just can't seem to get a grip on what he wants to do. About you, or his future. I do care for you, Jo Ann, more than any man should."

"More than working cattle . . . or shepherding your Hashknife waddies?"

He smiled back, reached for the cup again, withdrew his hand and said, "Lots more."

"Bill, I've always been . . . sort of headstrong. And you must agree that I've been patient with you . . . hoping that ours will be more than just seeing each other here at the cafe . . . or a date once in while."

"I feel the same way, I guess."

"Have you saved any money?"

"Some."

From an apron pocket she withdrew a folded envelope. "That'll help. The Merryfield General Store has gotten in some jewelry, rings and things like that. Take this money and head over there, Mr. Lowman, and buy me one."

"One, what?"

"An engagement ring!"

All the segundo could do was straighten up in the booth as silence fell upon the other booths and nearby tables, and somehow he found himself being handed the envelope and wedging on his hat as he left the Oyster Grotto. When he returned, about a half hour later, the ring he slipped upon the finger of Jo Ann Newkirk made him an engaged man. Somehow, it made him forget a lot of things.

Only when a cowboy shoved the door open to announce that Johnny Crowheart had escaped, did the flush of happiness leave the segundo, for only he knew Crowheart was innocent. He left with the other customers to see what had happened, as the town marshal gestured excitedly where he stood surveying the open door of the shack. Lowman got there just in time to hear Windom Brown say that a young woman had helped Crowheart escape.

"So we gotta form a posse," the town marshal exclaimed.

"That should be left up to that U.S. marshal. After all, it was him bringing in Crowheart."

"Windom, you said Crowheart headed out of town around ten last night. If so, his tracks would be covered by this snow. I doubt if he'll get far. Wonder who that woman was?"

"We know, don't we, Bill," said Arty Lamar. "Carrie Morgan got him out. I'll tell you this, I get Crowheart in my sights he's going down."

"Seems you two never hit it off too much," said Lowman.

"What's that supposed to mean?"

"I know why she got Crowheart out of jail. I also know he never killed Darin Murdock. So, if you want to keep on working for the Hashknife, Lamar, you won't go gunning for Johnny." Bill Lowman strode

208

away, knowing from the talk coming from the men clustered near the shack that hunting down Johnny Crowheart was going to be left to Marshal Con Tillison.

Another matter of concern was the weather. Here it was, just heading into October, and it seemed winter was making that first chilling push down from the Arctic regions. The Hashknife was still overstocked with cattle. All summer they'd been grazing on range suffering the effects of a virtual drought. Though there had been some rainfall, the long dry spells between these occasional thundershowers had taken their toll on the grasslands. They would have to cut out a lot more cattle, as would other ranches, then probably be forced to take a lower price for this livestock, but any profit at all was better than seeing a lot of cattle go under if these snowstorms kept up.

Swinging his thoughts back to Crowheart, he just had a hunch that the waddy and Carrie Morgan were making plans right about now to seek out Yakima Pierce, or failing that, her brothers, in an attempt to clear Johnny's name. There were also those other outlaws. Which meant the two youngsters were taking on a chore that could see both of them killed.

"Bill," Jo Ann Newkirk called out to him. "What's going on?"

"Just that Crowheart got away is about all."

"Guess who just came in on the morning train from Dickinson. Territorial Judge Jason Caruthers. And mad as a wet hen because Marshal Tillison wasn't here and Crowheart had broke jail."

"About all he can do now is make a snowman."

"Well, his honor said that Medora should build a

jail pronto and elect a sheriff even faster. Guess he's heading back to Dickinson on the first available train. When are you leaving?"

"Thought about leaving when this snow let up. Seems it has."

"Couldn't you wait until tomorrow?"

"Jo Ann, I am worried about leaving our other herds undermanned. You never know when rustlers will hit."

"I understand. But I feel we have to talk . . . about us. About our future."

"Reckon I owe you that, alright. It's warming some; should be maybe in the forties or fifties tomorrow. You know, though, that sudden move of yours took some of the starch out of me. Never been engaged before."

"For my sake I hope it isn't a long one. I'm making supper at my place tonight, around seven. Be there, Bill Lowman."

Chapter Sixteen

A spell of warmer weather hitting the Badlands caused many ranchers to believe that it would be another mild winter. Some of them let their cattle begin drifting. But at the Hashknife it had been decided to ship to market another five hundred head, a decision made by Jake Murdock at the insistence of his segundo.

It was five days after Bill Lowman had returned from Medora. Some of the waddies couldn't help joshing their foreman about his getting engaged, and he merely smiled and let them have their fun. He couldn't help thinking about Johnny Crowheart. Where would they go, the waddy and Carrie Morgan? If, as he'd suspected before, Johnny had hopes of going after Yakima Pierce, both Johnny and the girl could be dead. He hadn't discussed with Jake Murdock what Carrie had told him, nor would he for the moment. Settled in the owner of the Hashknife was a deep well of bitterness, and Murdock had lost a little weight. However, the bossman had picked up some of the slack and came out to check on the cattle at various times.

The haze, Lowman couldn't help noticing, which

had hung over the Badlands since autumn, was lifting, and by day or night sun dogs glowed around the moon and sun. The sky was trying to tell the segundo something. Perhaps that he'd better get those cattle down to Medora soon or not at all. Later that day, as Bill Lowman came riding into the home range, it was to find the Hashknife had some unexpected visitors.

"Out looking for Crowheart?" Lowman asked U.S. Marshal Con Tillison standing at one of the corrals with Jake Murdock and his deputies.

"We'll get him. Right now I'm discussing a more important matter with your boss. In the next couple of days Turk Widen and his hardcases are going to hit your herd. Seems my scouting out some of the places these outlaws have been using as hideouts paid off. I'm talking, here, about the Ezra Morgan place up near Caprock Coulee."

"How'd you figure Morgan to be involved in this?"

"From all that bar talk taking place down in Little Misery. It's his no-account sons I'm after. I could have arrested Ezra. In exchange for not doing so he spilled the beans about the rustling. And about them coming in to hit your herd."

"What else did Ezra tell you?"

"What else could he tell me," said Marshal Tillison, as Lowman removed the saddle from his horse and draped it on a corral pole.

"If you would have asked him, Marshal, you would have been told that Johnny Crowheart isn't a murderer."

"Dammit," blazed Jake Murdock, "he killed my boy . . . and he's gonna hang for it. You should'a let me do the job when we had him."

212

"Just what do you know, Lowman?"

"Carrie Morgan came down here. Told me it was Yakima Pierce killing Jake's son, them others. I believe her."

"She said that just to protect Crowheart."

"If I had to choose between taking Yakima's word or hers, she'd win hands down," said the segundo. "Jake, you might as well hear the rest of what I found out. Your son was telling the Widen gang where the ranchers were summering their cattle. He was getting paid to do this. It was his whole idea in the first place."

"Damn you, Lowman!" Jake Murdock lashed out and backhanded his segundo across the face, and if he had been carrying a handgun, he would have gone for that next. "My son had his faults, damn you! But he wasn't mixed up with the likes of the Morgan brothers or Yakima Pierce. Now, get off my ranch before I kill you." Trembling from the emotion of what he'd done, and shaken also by what he'd learned, Jake Murdock swung around and headed for the main house.

Bill Lowman could still feel the impact of the blow, and he grimaced at the marshal. "When the truth comes out it hurts all of us. Anyway, I guess that's it for me out here."

"What about those rustlers?"

"That's your worry now, Tillison. I've just been fired."

"Fired or not, Lowman, I need your help. Murdock, he seems to have given up, wasn't too receptive to my being here. Sounded downright skeptical when I told him about those rustlers trying for his cattle."

213

"Even with what happened, I guess after all these years I owe Jake something. You say they'll hit most anytime?"

"Ezra Morgan told me he's pulling out for Oregon before those outlaws get back. I told him, 'You do that, and for damned sure I'll follow you there and make sure you hang along with your sons.' Jake Murdock's son told them where that herd was going to be held—"

"North of the Achenback Hills."

"I want them, bad. What I also learned is that Turk Widen had been having other rustlers sell what they steal to him. There's this setup he has up along the Missouri River, in them breaks. He holds these cattle or horses until those Metis show up. This summer he's made a bundle off this rustling . . . along with killing a few cowhands. Well, Lowman, what's it to be?"

"Just this, Tillison, that it wasn't Crowheart killing Jake's son. I expect he's out there someplace waiting to have a go at getting Yakima Pierce. I want the charges against Crowheart dropped, and Carrie Morgan for breaking him out of jail."

"You've got it. But how do we know if she's lying? That knife of Crowheart's is pretty strong evidence."

"She mentioned one of her brothers, Trace, staying behind to watch Yakima use his knife on Jake's son."

"Trace'll hang with the others then."

Lowman raised his eyes to the afternoon sun. "If we leave now, we'll get there around sundown. What about Jake; is he going along?"

"I expect he is."

"Marshal, you wait for Jake. I'll take the half-dozen hands working here at the home place with me.

There's another dozen men with that herd."

"Those rustlers will shy away if they find too many men guarding the cattle. Pull off some, and let them rustlers come in before you make your play. I doubt if any of them will give up. Just so you know what to expect."

Later, riding among six Hashknife waddies, Bill Lowman felt the warming wind striking out. During the day greyish clouds had been building up to the southwest, from which direction came the low rumble of thunder, and one of the hands remarked that it might rain. Lowman had seen no need to tell the men of his being let go by Jake Murdock. And he'd asked Marshal Tillison not to tell the rancher he'd be one of those waiting down at the Achenback Hills for the Widen gang to show.

"There'll probably be gunplay," Lowman explained.

"Maybe so, Bill, but we're tired of what's been going on. Just hope we can end this rustling once and for all."

"If it's at all possible, I want Trace Morgan alive."

They all fell silent after that, letting their horses settle into a ground-eating canter, with the Little Missouri showing southward and those storm clouds building up and seeming to be aimed at where they were going: the Achenback Hills.

"Just where did your daughter go, Ezra?"

"Stole my sixgun and horse and skedaddled," he said bitterly.

"That waddy, Crowheart's, been arrested," Turk Widen said. He allowed a lazy smile to show and speared another pork chop from the platter on the table. Gathered around the table were all of the Morgans, Widen and the three remaining members of his gang, and of course, Yakima Pierce eating sullenly and more than the others.

Mack Blackthorn muttered, "It worries me your daughter not being here. Is there something we should know?"

Despite the heat coming from the pot-bellied stove, a sudden chill spread over Ezra Morgan, and he blustered, "She's been mooning over somebody, probably that no-account Crowheart. But I'll whale her badly when she gets back. Anyway, Blackthorn, my daughter's no concern of yours."

"Ezra's right," said Turk Widen. "Lay off, Mack."

"While you was gone," Ezra said slyly, "went down to Medora for supplies. Chanced upon a big herd of Hashknife cattle being held down amongst the Achenback Hills."

"I know the place, Pa," piped up Abe Morgan.

"As I was a-telling you," continued the elder Morgan, "it seems from the way they was cutting out cattle they planned another trail drive to Medora. Prime beef there, I tell you."

"How many cowpunchers did you see?"

"I figure around ten, eleven."

"Easy pickings," said George Ramshorn. "Besides, it appears that it might snow tonight. Any storm will cover our tracks."

Using his finger to work a hunk of pork wedged between two teeth, Kelly Bartow said, "Feels more like it's gonna rain."

"Yakima, I've heard from everyone else?"

"You say Crowheart's jailed down in Medora." He scratched at his unkempt beard with a greasy hand. "After we rustle them cattle, that's where I'm heading." His eyes contained a strange and deadly glitter that caused everyone there to bend to the task of eating.

"Joe Bob, pass me that whiskey bottle."

"Get your own bottle!" he snarled.

"Tarnation, Joe Bob, pass that bottle to your brother." Rising, Ezra Morgan grabbed the empty meat platter and went into the kitchen, where in a frying pan more pork chops were browning. As soon as everyone trailed out for the Achenback Hills and those Hashknife cattle, he was packing his things and leaving permanentlike. He felt a little giddy, mostly from fear and because he was coming down with a cold. From the cramped living room came the bragging talk of the outlaws, and when a sudden gust of wind rattled a window pane, his eyes swiveled to look out through it. A storm was brewing, one blending the forces of late autumn when icy rain would come down with coming winter. His bones had been aching for about a month now, a sure sign of a weather change, and he could read sky sign as well as the next man. Death was etched up there, maybe his, most certainly these outlaws and his sons if they kept up this thieving.

About an hour after Ezra Morgan had fed the outlaws, one of them, Turk Widen, came in to say they were leaving. He passed to the wolfer a crumbled wad of money, and nodding around a smile, he left with the others.

Ever since the unexpected appearance of U.S. Marshal Con Tillison, Ezra Morgan had stowed what he wanted to take along in packs hidden out in one of the sheds. First he retrieved from under a loose floorboard in his bedroom a leather pouch bulging with money. Putting on his outer garments, he didn't bother taking a final nostalgic look around at the sod house he'd built as he went out the front door and ambled to the corral. In one hand he carried his Winchester, still not feeling comfortable about not having his handgun snugged down at his hip.

"I'll tan her proper she ever shows up again," muttered Ezra Morgan as he set about saddling the horse he'd be riding, one bearing the 777 brand. He would take another saddle horse, and a pack horse, which he roped and brought out of the corral and over to the shed. A couple of hard day's riding, he reckoned, would put this place and the Badlands far behind. Briefly, he centered his thoughts on his daughter as he adjusted the pack saddle on the horse. Probably mooning after that no-account waddy. But at least them outlaws didn't get their dirty paws on her. Now he felt more than saw a day shadow drifting in from behind, with the whickering of a horse sending him spinning for the rifle he'd set against the shed door.

One of Yakima Pierce's big hands clamped on the wolfer's neck before his hunting knife plunged hilt-deep into Ezra Morgan's back. The blade must have severed the spinal cord, for Ezra didn't even cry out but went limp. Pulling out his knife, Yakima brought it around and slit the wolfer's throat to make sure he was dead. Then he dragged Ezra Morgan into the shed, with his eyes filming over as he scalped his victim while muttering in Sioux. If he had had more time, Yakima would have skinned the wolfer while he was still alive, but the scalp he tied at his belt served to calm down his lust for blood as he lit a match and tossed it onto some old straw stacked against a wall. Finding his horse, he headed south to catch up with the others, and in doing so, passed Carrie Morgan hidden in a copse of elm trees.

As the buffalo hunter loped his horse over a distant rise, flames licking at the shed sent Carrie into the saddle and heading her horse that way. Dismounting at the run, she called out, "Pa! Pa, the shed's on fire!" She groped through the billowing smoke and stopped when she saw what Yakima had done to her father. Now the flames drove her out of the ramshackle building, and all Carrie Morgan could do was stand there, her heart aching for her father but unable to shed any tears.

"Why?" she cried out to the buffeting wind. "Why are some men such animals?" She stood watching until the walls gave way and the building began crumbling, and then a very frightened Carrie Morgan made for the house.

Inside the sod building that had been her home, Carrie was afraid to make a fire or light a lamp. She was still numbed by what had happened. After a while it dawned on her that Yakima Pierce had headed south, and perhaps those other horsemen she'd sighted when coming in from the same direction had been her brothers and those outlaws. If they were, Johnny had been right, that the Widen gang was going to go after those Hashknife cattle held down by the Achenback Hills.

"His boss . . . Bill Lowman." Realizing the only way she could keep the man she loved from getting gunned down was to ride as hard as she could for the Hashknife Spread, Carrie shoved open the door and ran toward her horse. Now, if only she could get there in time.

Chapter Seventeen

Most of Johnny Crowheart's worries had been for Carrie taking off by her lonesome. It had only struck him after she'd ridden out that he might not see her again. How much did she mean to him, a cowpoke leading a wandering tumbleweed kind of life? Just that a woman such as Carrie Morgan only came along once in a man's lifetime. Spending a night with her at that abandoned cabin, and a few nights thereafter, as they managed to keep ahead of that pursuing U.S. marshal, had sort of wedded them together. But make no mistake about it, they were still in that hand-holding stage.

This was the second night he'd been camped on an escarpment in the Achenback Hills. The cautious campfire he'd made had served to warm Crowheart's food while leaving him wishing for the bunkhouse back at the Hashknife. Wistfully, too his thoughts sent him back to the night Carrie Morgan had bailed him out of that jail in Medora:

"Just not used to snow."

"Stick around awhile, Crowheart."

Having just bedded their horses down in a shed behind the log cabin, the waddy and the sodbuster's daughter had come into the cabin to shake the snow from their clothing and make a warming fire. While

221

he tended to that, Carrie rummaged around in her saddlebags to produce that first shared supper. Outside, the wintry storm kept driving southward and wiping out the tracks left by their horses. Later came a few probing questions from Carrie Morgan that left Johnny's mind reeling.

"Have I ever been with a woman?"

"Well, Crowheart, have you?"

"There's been a couple of saloon girls — but nothing serious."

"I won't count that against you."

Right about then Johnny knew better than to ask if she had ever been serious about another man, and even if she had, about Carrie there was a sense of pureness, telling him it would take a marriage vow before a man would have his way with her. And here he was, sharing this night and a lonesome cabin with the woman he loved.

"As to why I got you out, Crowheart, just didn't want to see you get strung up for something Yakima Pierce did."

"I want to find him. See him hang for what he done to Jake's son and only the Good Lord knows how many others." Then he saw the sad glimmer in her eyes. "I know, your brothers got themselves mixed up in this. But, Carrie, it wouldn't be right them not getting arrested, too."

"They're kin, alright. My blood and flesh. But gone bad, Johnny, gone so terribly bad."

"You mentioned Trace being there when Yakima killed Darin Murdock."

"Suppose Trace is just as guilty. Sometimes, Crowheart, I feel all that has happened isn't fair. Us living like this, grubbing it out. Pa not caring what my brothers do, or if they kill someone. Me . . . me just there to remind Pa of what my mother did. Then I had to have the misfortune of falling in love with you, Crowheart."

"That's bad luck for sure."

"Johnny, why don't we just forget what's going on here. Just leave. We can head west. Oh, I'd just love to see that California. Just love to get a fresh start in life. Just you and me."

"You'd be cutting out, Carrie, with a man wanted for murder. Sooner or later they'd find us. I got no choice but to clear my name. Carrie, I . . . when you talk of going westward with me over them sky-touchin' Rockies, does this mean you'll marry me?"

"If you'll have me."

It was Carrie Morgan that came over to the man she loved and drew him close, touching her lips to Johnny Crowheart's. It was a lingering kiss. For a while the storm and their troubles vanished. Their hands touched faces, and hair, their eyes reaching out in a kind of wonderment and tingling promise of what was to come. And, finally, it was the wise woman-logic of Carrie Morgan that decided their fate.

"Johnny, you're right, we can't run away from this." Tears welled from her eyes, which he brushed away. "It's something both of us have to face up to."

"You mean, going after Yakima—"

"That, Crowheart, and our destiny."

"Getting late."

"I know."

"We've got two bedrolls." His smile suggested other

things.

But at Carrie's look, he decided to bed down on the other side of the stove.

The next few days found them riding deeper into the snowscaped reaches of the Badlands. Though the storm had let up, it was still blustery cold out. Once in a while they caught glimpses of riders far to the south, and it was necessary for them to keep on the dodge, while angling up to the Hashknife as Crowheart had remembered being told by Bill Lowman about a big herd of cattle being gathered in the shadow of the Achenback hills. They traveled with Carrie's worry about her family separating them. Then Johnny Crowheart spoke these warning words: "Okay, you overheard them saying they would rustle some Hashknife cattle."

"They're going to, Johnny. But Turk Widen wanted to head up along the Missouri first."

"Carrie, you just ease in there. Those outlaws won't believe you came down just to get me out of jail. No telling what Widen, or that Yakima will do."

"You act as if we're already married, Crowheart. If they're at our place, I'll come back down here. And you, you be careful."

Johnny Crowheart had been awfully careful, hunkered down as he'd been on this elevation giving him a long view of the line shack located by a natural spring, while thirsting for some of that pure water and for them outlaws to show. He'd tallied the herd gathered below the hills at around three thousand head, the Hashknife waddies cutting out marketable cattle to form a smaller herd, which they'd trail out to Medora. On the second day of Johnny's vigil it warmed into the high fifties, and higher the third day, however the sky was still hazy as though a prairie fire had been raging out of control. And the trees were uncertain of what was going on, some of them, cottonwoods mostly, shedded down to bare limb, the smaller trees such as willows and cedars heavy with leaf and bowed some by the latest snowfall. Around noon the sky began clouding up, swift-moving clouds have no discernible shape and smoking to the northeast as if late for a hanging. It was around nightfall that he spotted other riders coming in, and he got excited. At last, the Widen gang was here! It took less than ten minutes for him to calm down when he made out that it was Bill Lowman and five other Hashknife waddies. After congregating by the line shack, a wondering Johnny Crowheart saw them scattering out to various hiding places, staying close enough to keep an eye on the herd, now being guarded by only five men.

"Now what?"

He puzzled over that for a spell while his jaws kept working on an unyielding hunk of dried beef. He hadn't seen that U.S. marshal for at least three days. And before that, Marshal Con Tillison had been up in these parts looking for outlaw hideouts. Could it be possible that the marshal had passed the day with Ezra Morgan? A rumble of thunder like a gatling gun letting go brought Johnny's surprised eyes to the southwest. Another crescendo of thunder let go, while lightning bolts seemed to be working through the low, dark and ominous clouds and crackling and lancing groundward. The herd felt the presence of the storm, too, and it began stirring and milling as daylight edged away to find a safer place to cast its dim light. Now the leading edge of the storm pressed closer to the Achenback Hills throwing icy rain before it, and Crowheart hustled for his rain slicker.

When he eased back to the rim of the escarpment, it was to find riders coming in hard and fanning out, firing at those shepherding the Hashknife cattle. Flame spurted from roaring guns as Johnny sprang toward his horse and vaulted into the saddle. Even at this distance, of around a half-mile, he'd picked out the buffalo hunter.

As he brought his bronc recklessly down the slope of the hill, the cattle surged up along the wide reaches of the draw, and it wasn't the gunfire so much as it was fox-fire flung by the storm coming overhead. For a moment, Crowheart reined up some and stared in awe at the phosphorescent light glowing on the horn-tips and ears of the stampeding cattle.

Northeast of the Achenback Hills, and unaware of the presence of Johnny Crowheart, the men with Bill Lowman, astride their horses, came in pouring rifle fire at the rustlers. They parted as the cattle pounded at them and passed, as snow mixed with the rain and lay white on the ground. Some men were going down: two Hashknife cowpunchers, Kelly Bartow gutshot and two of the Morgan brothers gunned out of their saddles. Outlaw George Ramshorn got it next, a rifle slug in the back of the head. He dropped in the path of the onrushing cattle and simply disappeared.

For the segundo Bill Lowman there came a numbing pain, but somehow he clung to the saddle and his rifle, not realizing just how bad he'd been hit. When he fell, there was a surprised look on his face. The others with him kept pounding after the cattle and outlaws, not knowing that their segundo had gone down.

Johnny Crowheart, riding hard at a veering run that brought him closing on those at the front of the herd of stampeding cattle, Yakima Pierce and Turk Widen, knew that Widen had been hit when he suddenly lurched in the saddle. Then, a wall of rain-slogged snow caused him to lose sight of the outlaws, but he could have sworn that Turk Widen had fallen from his horse. When Johnny's horse shied away from lightning spearing down so close he could feel it all but singeing his hat, he pulled up short and stared wildly at the lowered sky.

"Can't stop now," he told himself, and he jabbed his spurs to bring his bronc after Yakima Pierce.

The lowering visibility caused the herd to slow down and begin drifting aimlessly. Still, Crowheart kept pressing his horse to the north. The only place the buffalo hunter would head was Ezra Morgan's. And just where was Carrie? The fear that Yakima would run into her kept Johnny saddlebound and at the mercy of the storm pouring out thunderclaps, jagged lightning and freezing snowflakes.

"I hear gunfire!"

"That means Ezra Morgan was right!" exclaimed Marshal Con Tillison. He brought his horse into a gallop with the others as they closed on the Achenback Hills shrouded by the storm. Coming to them also was the drumming of the runaway herd. Sweeping out of a draw, they reined up four abreast as a rifle boomed, followed by a rider fanning a handgun so fast that the report of its chamber being emptied echoed as one slug. Lightning flaring, showed the owner of that handgun to be an outlaw, a fact shouted out by Jake Murdock.

U.S. Marshal Con Tillison's response came fast and to the report of his rifle crackling, and outlaw Mack Blackthorn went down under the impact of a lead slug breaking the back of his neck.

"Aimed for his chest," muttered the marshal. "Let's move in . . . slowly."

Using the line shack as a homing point, the latest arrivals swung to the north and soon came upon cattle which had gone down, along with the bodies of a Hashknife waddy and an outlaw, Abe Morgan, sprawled lifelessly about five yards apart. Farther on, a horse neighed its pain, and grimacing with his own pain and anger, Jake Murdock squeezed off a shot that took the suffering horse in the head.

"Jake, that you?"

"It's me, Lamar."

"I captured me one of them outlaws. One of them rotten Morgan brothers. Me and Si Reese caught him."

They reined up and stared down at the two waddies hovering over Trace Morgan clutching at a broken left arm, and the ominous crackle of Jake Murdock levering a shell into the breech of his Remington caused Marshal Tillison to move closer and grab the barrel of the rifle.

"I want this one alive."

"I want the dirty scum dead!"

"I'm the law out here, Murdock. Rustler or not, you shoot this man and I'll see you in jail."

"Over here!" someone called out just to the north of them. "I've found Bill Lowman. Damn . . . he's sure bleeding."

"Lowman?"

"Yup, Mr. Murdock, it was his idea coming out here. Somehow I don't think it was all that good a notion." Glaring at the rancher, Marshal Tillison and his deputies brought their horses into a canter.

Finally, Jake Murdock said grimly, "Don't let him get away." He spurred after the lawmen and swung to the ground but could only stand there and stare in surprise at the man he'd fired.

The waddy tending to the segundo looked up at the rancher and said through pleading eyes, "I don't know, Jake, he's hurt bad. Took that slug just above the heart."

Crouching down, Murdock reached out a tentative hand and placed it on Bill Lowman's shoulder. Any anger he felt toward the man who'd been his lifelong friend was swept away, by the storm and the knowledge that the segundo had more craw and loyalty than a man like Jake Murdock deserved. In a voice breaking with sorrow, and the stampede forgotten, he said, "We'll ease him over to the line shack. Reese, you take my horse and ride like hell for Medora and Doc Henderson. It'll take you all night, and maybe some more, but if you have to kill the horse, do so."

"Yessir, Mr. Murdock. I won't let you down." Climbing into the saddle, Si Reese was soon lost in the thick curtain of snow beginning to deepen on the Badlands.

Chapter Eighteen

A man could only push himself so far in weather like this, and for Johnny Crowheart it came time to hole up when his bronc staggered going down into a coulee and went to its knees. He left the saddle, tightened his grip on the reins, and said in a voice trembling with cold, "Easy, now, easy." It could have been the middle of the night, or coming onto dawning, for all he knew or cared, his only concern now was to get down under an overhang and out of this driving snow.

Pressing through willows caked with icicles and then under some cedar trees still bearing leafs, the force of the wind went away, as did the needle-edged snow. He almost walked into a coulee wall rising straight up, and groped along it. When it suddenly fell away, there was a sort of cave cut deep into the loamy soil. He brought the horse in, and all it could do was stand with its head down and breathe heavily through its flaring nostrils as Johnny unsaddled it. He made sure it wouldn't get away by tying the reins to a hunk of tree that had wedged into the deep opening in the coulee wall. Then all he could do was crawl into his bedroll and try to warm himself and get some sleep. Thinking of Carrie, and the man he was chas-

231

ing, kept him awake, and all of a sudden he dropped off.

What awakened Crowheart was the silence. Opening his eyes, he discovered the sun was just coming up and the sky was a dazzling blue, a high sky that brought him out of the bedroll and seeking wood to make a fire. He found that it had been a driving snow, the wind sweeping it into scattered drifts and crusting underfoot as he moved about. Once the fire was going, he hunkered down by it. The bronc began stirring about and edged closer to Crowheart, and he said tiredly, "Yup, hoss, I'll get you some water. But for now, help yourself to some of that grass."

He rode out within the half-hour, by the sun to the north, and when he came to a creek, he broke the thin plate of ice with his boot so that the horse could drink. He felt better now that the storm was over, and riding on again, began seeking out the landmarks he knew, since it was his notion he was on that section of land to the west of Squaw Creek. As for Yakima Pierce, the man had probably sought out his own shelter last night.

Later that morning Crowheart picked up the trail of two horses heading north as he was, and he followed them. A short time later he spotted blood staining a snowy patch of ground, and it came to him that Turk Widen was still alive. For certain they'd need shelter now, and that meant the Morgan place. Fearing the worst, Johnny brought the bronc into a faster gait.

About three miles south of Caprock Coulee, and as he stopped to rest his horse, smoke suddenly stabbed the sky from that general direction, which soon thickened into a black pillar. "They must have set fire to the place. If they've harmed Carrie!"

He forgot about resting the bronc and forced it into a headlong gallop. Then at last he was coming onto the approaches to Caprock Coulee, and rounding a bend in the wall, he caught sight of the Morgan house, a mass of flames, and the corral empty. Slowing his mount down, Johnny went in warily, his six-gun in hand. His eyes went past the burning house to a shed that showed recent signs of having been burned. He closed on the corral and swung his horse around in a circle while probing for signs of life, and then he shouted:

"Carrie, it's me, Johnny! It's okay!"

He waited there, and then he realized from this feeling he had that he was alone, and he brought his horse past the garden and over to the creek to let it slake its thirst. Refilling his canteen, Johnny pondered over his next move. It was obvious that Yakima Pierce and Widen wanted to keep heading north and get away from their pursuers, in this case, Johnny Crowheart. So all he had to do was pick up their trail. Ezra Morgan must have been with them, along with Carrie. She had spoken to him of her fear for the lusting Turk Widen, and that Yakima was also like-minded. As long as her father was there, the outlaws would probably keep their distance. Now it was time to check out the two sheds still untouched for some food and maybe some sweet feed for the bronc. In one of the sheds he found some potatoes and some vegetables collected from the garden, and hung up to smoke, a ham hock. He filled his saddlebags to bulging.

A circle ride of the buildings soon produced a trail

left by three horses, and Johnny exclaimed anxiously, "They must have killed Ezra Morgan and taken his daughter!" It didn't occur to Crowheart, not until two days later when he sighted two horsemen leading a packhorse in an angling ride toward the Missouri River, that Yakima or Turk Widen had killed the woman he loved. For where else could she be but in that burning house. And a need to exact revenge even as a pain touched his heart brought Crowheart onward under a sky hazing again.

"I tell you, Yakima, somebody's back there!"

"Could be, Turk. You want to hang back and get a shot at him?"

"No, damn you, we'll keep pressing on." The shoulder wound had been looked at by Yakima, who'd then affixed a crude bandage, and still in there was the slug that had struck Turk Widen. He was in a lot of pain, and in the two days since they'd left Caprock Coulee, the outlaw had been drinking steadily of Ezra Morgan's cheap whiskey. Their plan was to get to their camp west along the Missouri breaks, and from there make a break for Canada and lay low with the Metis. What worried Widen more than his shoulder wound was the buffalo hunter. Yakima Pierce wasn't noted for his loyal ways, or of having any other human virtue. And there was the money Widen had cached up by their hideout. The way he read it, he could survive this shoulder wound long enough to get up to Medicine Hat and have a real sawbones dig that slug out, but not too many more days with Yakima Pierce. It was there, plain in Widen's mind, Yakima meant to kill him for that money.

"Are you sure there's only one rider trailing us?" Widen asked.

"Just the one."

Widen's teeth clenched together when his horse stumbled on the slippery ground, then he nodded at an outcropping. "We should try to get up there and set an ambush."

"Only a mountain sheep could make that climb," Yakima said sullenly. "Up ahead, there's some trees growing on that rise. We'll take him out there." In passing through the draw they scared up an old longhorn bull, which hooked at them with those curving horns before plunging back into the underbrush. Yakima brought his horse plunging over a fallen tree encrusted with icy snow, and Turk Widen had no choice but to do the same. When his horse landed on the northern side, the outlaw cursed back the pain. They brought their spent horses onto the rise and drew up under trees having their roots planted deep in scoria. Clumsily the buffalo hunter came out of the saddle. He eased the Sharps 50-90 out of the fringed gun case, and then Yakima passed his reins to Turk Widen, who brought their horses back amongst the trees.

Yakima Pierce crouching in under a cedar tree sent icy snow clinging to its branches falling to the ground, and after placing the barrel on a lower branch to steady it, he dropped to his knees and stared eastward along the only coulee, which tapered down toward brush growing along a creek, and where their backtrail lay. He shoved a brass cartridge into the chamber as Widen hunkered in beside him, and Yakima said,

"By nightfall we should be at the hideout. Once I get that slug out, we'd best trail up to Canady."

"Why the hurry?"

"Another storm hits we'll be snowed in there for a long spell."

"There, he's just dropping down into the coulee. Wonder who it is."

"Don't matter none does it 'cause he'll be dead in about two minutes."

The man they were watching was still some distance away, perhaps a mile-and-a-half, and Yakima waited until he came a lot closer but still out of Winchester range before he brought up the Big Fifty Sharps and sighted down the metallic-blue barrel.

Turk Widen blinked when the Sharps cut loose, and he exclaimed, "You got his horse; should have let him come closer."

"No place to hide down there." Calmly the buffalo hunter reloaded the Sharps, eased the barrel over a notch and placed another slug where the man following them had taken shelter.

That slug slammed into the tree above Johnny Crowheart and gouged out a large hunk of wood. Out in the open, his bronc had taken the first heavy slug directly in its chest, killing it where it stood and dropping it down so hard he'd come tumbling forward to land on its head. From there he'd scrambled into the trees. Now he sprinted closer to the coulee wall and dove behind a boulder as another slug came crackling his way. He lay there until the day began dimming into twilight. By then he realized those he'd been following had ridden on. Trudging out to the dead horse, he retrieved his rifle, bedroll and saddlebags.

As Johnny picked up the trail of the outlaws, he knew caution should have been the order of the day. Though he'd been keeping out of rifle range, Johnny had forgotten about that buffer gun of Yakima's, and that another careless move might be his last. When he came to a fallen tree blocking his progress, he crawled over it and just beyond came upon a few beads of blood beside a hoof mark. They would have to hole up and treat Turk Widen's wound. But now he was afoot and falling behind with every passing minute, along with finding that struggling through an occasional drift or plain walking was a chore in his high-heeled boots. Coming out of the coulee, he caught his first glimpse of the breaks coursing to the west along the Missouri River.

Now he had a choice to make: get moving after Yakima or go down to lower ground and settle in for the night. But, thinking on it, Johnny realized that to survive afoot he would have to head northward into the breaks and hunt up some shelter. Veering that way, he went down a patch of barren ground and toward the river along a shallow draw, to drop into a deeper one as it became darker out, and colder. Still marking the sky were those sun dogs, and this eerie haze, and there was no moon to help Johnny in his search of shelter, though stars were spiking twinkling holes in the dome above. Sometime later, three hours or more, he came laboring down a narrow game trail slicing around trees and into a small clearing to find in it a camp showing recent signs of use. He held there for a while, with the increasing chill of night telling him to go on in, and finally Crowheart did, at a slow walk. The pole gate of a corral stood open, and on it he saw that someone had left a hackamore. A close look at it told Crowheart it had been used lately—probably by one of the outlaws said to be infesting these parts.

"Feet," he said wearily, "I know you're aching. Soon's I get a fire going these boots are coming off."

The cabin was a crude affair with the logs that formed its walls not cut off but sticking out from the corners and low-sloped, and to Crowheart's surprise, it contained a fireplace built up along one wall and provisions, which would only mean those who'd put them here had plans of coming back. Johnny's first order of business was a fire. And when flames were eating at wood in the fireplace, he took an old bucket and went in search of water, which came from a creek pouring cold water into the Missouri just beyond the clearing. Back in the cabin, he let some water heat over the fire as he duffed his boots and outer clothing. His rummaging about had produced a bearskin robe, which he wrapped about his body as he eased down by the fire and placed his feet in the warm bucket of water. One of the boots had split open, and his foot was raw and swollen. Food would come later, the little he'd brought along, and a lot more cached in a bin.

Drowsiness overcame Johnny as he sat there, while out beyond the walls of the log cabin a sky change was taking place. The haze was being slowly eased away by a whitish cloud wall coming over the northern horizon. On it came, with almost no wind pushing it from behind, until onto the Missouri breaks came this icy sting pricking at the nostrils of cattle and horses, a white snow powdered so fine and soft that it hovered until past midnight in the windless air before settling. Then the temperature began dropping well past the zero mark, and along toward morning out of Canada there came a sudden gale blowing curtains of snow before it. This was no ground blizzard where the sky was clear but a storm heavily-laden with cloud.

The storm raging at the cabin brought Crowheart out from under the buffalo robe and to the front door. He yanked it open to find the opening blocked by a drift reaching up to seal off the entrance. With a surprised grimace he closed the door and went sleepily over to start some wood burning in the fireplace. This, he soon found, was just one of the many storms that would keep him a virtual prisoner here, and as the wintry days of November marched through the Badlands, he could only think of avenging Carrie Morgan. To pass the time he cut pieces out of a buffalo robe and made a pair of shoes, and a fur cap and mittens. To get firewood he dared only venture out a short distance into the thick woods. He let his beard and hair grow, and sometimes his thoughts took to wandering so much that Crowheart felt he'd become crazed as Yakima Pierce.

Then, as though divined by a providential God, sometime in December came a brief spell of Indian summer, raising the temperature into the fifties and causing snowmelt. And it brought Johnny Crowheart away from the cabin and to the west along the Missouri River in search of those he'd vowed to kill.

Stowed under a bunk in the cabin, he had come across a pair of snowshoes and gotten accustomed to them while out looking for wood or game. He had no way of knowing that the snowshoes were a legacy left long ago by a woodcutter. From the idle chatter of the

Hashknife waddies, he'd found out that threading along the Missouri River banks were places such as he'd just left, and he felt certain that Yakima Pierce was holed up in one of them. As a matter of fact, Crowheart stole past clearings in which a few sagging roofs showed above the deep snow, and riverward, the Missouri no longer growled as the ice had frozen into a solid and thick sheet layered with snowfall after snowfall.

The going for Crowheart had been slow, as he was using muscles gone soft from lurking in that cabin, with even the weight of his rifle and the pack slung to his back tiring him. On the third day of his quest, he had just cleared still another clump of trees when there it was, a thin tendril of smoke curling skyward just around a bend in the river.

Dropping to his knees in powdery snow to take a breather, he kept his eyes on the column of smoke. It could be an outlaw gang or even some Indians who'd cut out from Fort Yates, and remembering that haste had almost gotten him killed before, Johnny made certain that a shell was lodged in the breech of his rifle before he brought his snowshoes plaining a jogging trail westward.

He kept to the high river bluffs instead of going down to travel along the narrow stretch of bank bending to the south now, and all of a sudden Crowheart was gazing at a cabin pouring out chimney smoke. In a corral were three horses. And tied to a tree was something that caused Johnny's blood to run cold.

"What in the—"

At this distance his first notion was that dangling from a high limb of a skeletal cedar was a mule deer

240

that had been skinned and hung up to dry. But there wasn't any member of the deer family on these Great Plains that had human hair and something resembling a man's face. For a moment he felt his mind go numb, and he froze there, amongst those pine trees sheltering him, only able to gape at what some human had done to another. The cabin door opened, and he stared at Yakima Pierce going out and over to the dead man dangling from the tree. In his hand he held that murderous hunting knife.

Crowheart pulled himself together and came ghosting down through the deep powdery snow covering the lowering slope, and closer, where the clear winter air brought to him the voice of the buffalo hunter, sort of strange sounding and tuned to an angry pitch.

"Widen, I know you got that money hid around here someplace. Now, I can go on and on cutting you up like this. But just tell me and I'll let you go." After a short wait, Yakima's knife sliced into the dead body of Turk Widen.

Fighting back his own fear, Crowheart came in closer, knowing that the buffalo hunter had gone around the bend, and he brought up the rifle and shouted, "Yakima, he's dead! Widen's dead!"

The buffalo hunter whirled around with flame spouting from the muzzle of the sixgun he'd pulled out of his holster. This was answered by the throatier roar of Johnny's rifle, the slug slapping into Yakima Pierce's thigh. Screaming in the Sioux tongue, he plunged through the thick snow toward Crowheart, who pumped enough shells at the crazed buffalo hunter to empty his rifle.

Then Yakima Pierce pulled up short and just

slumped over onto his face. Johnny Crowheart pulled out his handgun and was going to fire again, which he did, the slug plunking harmlessly into the ground and a sob escaping from his lips, he dropped to his knees in the snow, his body trembling from what had happened. Somehow he brought his eyes away from Yakima Pierce to the log cabin.

"Carrie?" he heard himself crying out, and breaking toward the cabin. One of the snowshoes came off, but he didn't seem to notice it was gone as he stumbled into the cabin. He called out again, and then Johnny Crowheart remembered that it was all over, and that Carrie was dead. He stood there, swaying some, with the stench of decayed meat and stale tobacco smoke jogging at his nostrils, and pain squinting his eyes. Finally it came to Johnny that he was suffering from cabin fever. The same thing could have happened to the buffalo hunter. Moving over, he slumped down at the table and lowered his head onto his arms, tired and bitter and so damnable lonely.

A long while later he stirred at the neighing of a horse. It took a moment for Crowheart to realize just where he was. He went outside and over to the corral, not wanting to tarry here but to simply head out where the air was cleaner and he would no longer be reminded of Yakima Pierce, or the Badlands, or of the woman he'd loved.

He picked out a sorrel not as gaunted as the others. After saddling the horse, he deposited his rifle in the scabbard and went to retrieve the snowshoes, which he knew would prove useful if the horse played out. Wearily he pulled himself onto the saddle. He sat there, in bright sunlight, and stared blankly at

Yakima, and then over at Turk Widen. He felt empty, as if all the emotion and hate had been burned out of him.

Somehow Johnny Crowheart found himself tracking to the south among the breaks weighed down with snow, and for the horse it proved to be tough going; but he went at a walk and kind of aimlessly. When the sun was angling at Johnny from the west he brought the sorrel onto a high ridge and stared with some awe at waves of snow billowing toward the distant horizon, with lines of violet shadow separating one white roller from another, and with others tinted into a deep blue as of an endless seascape broken by coral buttes.

"Winter," he said bitterly. "Winter of the blue snow."

Then, for some reason still unclear to him the young waddy set course to the southeast and the Hashknife Ranch, a long ride that could see him stretching hemp when he got there.

Chapter Nineteen

These warming days of Indian summer held steady, the snow melting to a depth of six inches, the balmy weather letting a lot of ranchers believe the worst was over. So they headed out to buy supplies or planned trips, and went out to check on cattle pawing the wet snow away from the trampled grass.

At the Hashknife Spread a noticeable change had taken place ever since Carrie Morgan had ridden in, going on a month now. Chiefly, this was caused by Jake Murdock. The confession from Trace Morgan that the buffalo hunter had killed his son had made the rancher do a lot of soul-searching. He regretted deeply beating Johnny Crowheart with that whip. Slowly he had overcome his suspicions that Carrie had been one of the rustlers. She was, he discovered in the close intimacy of his ranch house, not only very beautiful but possessing a will of her own. Perhaps this warmer weather had something to do with it, but in any case the rancher found himself chatting with her privately in the large and comfortable living room, a fire throwing out heat in the fieldstone fireplace and Carrie seated across from him at the oaken table. Adorning the walls were Spanish artifacts placed there by Rose Lopez. There were other mementos from Texas: a Henry rifle he'd bought down at Rosebud on the Brazos, some old Mex spurs with big rowels, a couple of sombreros, and on the mantle a wedding picture revealing that once upon a long ago time Jake Murdock had a full head of brownish hair. The high-raftered ceiling made the house seem larger.

All he could do for some time was stare at his big hands folded before him on the table, and when he looked at Carrie, it was to say quietly, "I'm sorry, Carry, this place is wearing on you."

"These storms have been hard on all of us."

"Your brother Trace," he said hesitantly, "will probably hang."

"That is something, Mr. Murdock, that I've come to accept."

"I know this has been wearing on you." He shifted to make himself more comfortable in the chair as Rose Lopez came out of the kitchen and set a tray on the living room table. "Now, Rose, that wasn't necessary. I've told you to take it easy . . . let Woody Hannagan do these things."

"Señor Jake, I have been taking it easy." She removed from the tray two cups and a coffee pot and plates holding slices of chocolate cake.

"Rose, I do declare, come spring I'll be round-bellied you keep this up." Through affectionate eyes he watched the older woman move slowly back into the kitchen. Then he filled their cups. "Young lady, what this powwow is all about is that I'm hoping you'll forgive me. What happened before . . . guess I was only trying to protect my son's name—now that I've had time to chew on it. This blinded me to your good intentions."

"Yes, one must be loyal to one's family."

"Something that you've been doing. I can only hope and pray that if Crowheart comes back, well, he can forgive me for what I did to him. But that'll be hard, the way I branded him an outlaw."

"Johnny's the forgiving kind, Mr. Murdock."

"Are you?"

"I . . . don't know. We . . . sodbusters have bad feelings about cowpokes. Never thought I'd fall in love with one."

"It was foolhardy Crowheart taking off after them outlaws by his lonesome. But like you told me before, Carrie, he thought you was up at your place. And if those outlaws haven't done Crowheart in, he might have gone down in one of these blizzards."

"Mr. Murdock, I won't let go of him until I know for certain Johnny's dead—and then maybe never."

"Glad you two are getting acquainted," called out Bill Lowman as he came into the room just ahead of Jo Ann Newkirk.

"You shouldn't be prowling around," the rancher scolded.

Jo Ann said, "Just another hardheaded Texan."

Upon learning that Bill Lowman had been wounded in that shootout with the Widen gang, Jo Ann Newkirk had rented a horse in Medora and ridden alone up here to the Hashknife. At the time she hadn't know of the bad blood between the man she was engaged to and the rancher. But at the time it wouldn't have made any difference, for upon arriving

247

here she found Bill Lowman fighting for his life, with Doc Henderson telling her that Lowman's chances were awfully slim. She had Felipe Lopez put another bed in Bill's room, and it was here she stayed while nursing him back to health. At times Rose Lopez or Carrie would spell her. And then one stormy day less than a week ago the segundo had come out of it, thirsty and hungry and surprised to see Jo Ann there. Later that day Jake Murdock had come into the room and asked both of them to stay on after they were married. He would turn over running the Hashknife to Lowman, not just as ranch foreman but as an equal partner. For Jo Ann Newkirk this had been a dream come true. However, on Lowman's part there had been some hesitancy, and she was wise enough not to force him into a decision.

Despite his protests to the contrary, she pulled out Bill's chair, and after he'd eased slowly onto it, Jo Ann came over and sat down beside Carrie Morgan. Between them had sprung up an easy friendship as they shared a closeness of having the men they loved imperiled, that chest wound of Lowman's finally healing, and Johnny Crowheart disappearing into the vast reaches of the winterbound Badlands.

A weather change a day later touched upon the Badlands, changing the slush into a slabby crust of ice. This forced hungry cattle to gnaw away at the hard snow covering until their muzzles were raw and swollen. Oftentimes the heavy weight of a steer would drop it through the hard-crusted snow injuring its legs, and unable to get out, the animal would soon perish.

Though Jake Murdock had kept on a few cowhands, their sustained effort to check on the cattle was hampered by the sub-zero cold and one storm after another. Murdock and Si Reese had just arrived back at the main buildings, cold and eager for some hot java, when out of the back door of the main house came Carrie Morgan. The blustery and yowling wind whipped at Carrie as she waved at the horsemen. To her it seemed the snow never stopped falling and forming sculpted drifts daily marching up the walls of the buildings. The cloud covering was a great smoky sheet draped just above the taller cottonwoods.

"How'd it go?"

Murdock yelled back, "Tarnable cold out there."

Then she swung her attention to the trail coming down from the north alongside Squaw Creek, something she'd been doing every day, for in her was a voice that told her the man she loved was still alive. Today the limits of her vision stretched out about a quarter of a mile, since daylight was no more than a pale lantern glow slowly being extinguished by the snowstorm.

For a moment a questioning light sparked in her eyes. Could it have been a black bear or elk she'd just seen? And Jake Murdock, watching her stare like that to the north, said to Si Reese, "Could be this storm's chased in something—"

"Yeah!" exclaimed the waddy. "Appears to be either a mountain man or trapper judging from those furs he's a-wearing! And coming in wearing snowshoes? That's something different?"

"Lordy," said Murdock. "Now that is a sight to behold!"

Before they could stir their horses into motion and

go out to help the fur-clad man, Carrie Morgan shouted so loud that the curtain of snow seemed to bend away.

"Johnny? I know it's you. Johnny!" She broke running that way as the man wearing snowshoes seemed to trip over something and go tumbling down into the snow to simply lay there.

The rancher and the cowpuncher came riding in, too, just as Carrie Morgan got there and dropped to her knees, crying and reaching down to bring the face of Johnny Crowheart's close to hers. Moaning her fear and mingled joy, she felt the hand of Jake Murdock touching her shoulder.

"Easy, girl, we'll bring him on in. My, that is some beard."

"Will . . . will he be alright?"

"Not if we keep jawing out here he won't."

250

Chapter Twenty

The turn of the year brought the month the Indians called "Moon of Cold-Exploding Trees" — and January 1887 came in cold, a time of almost constant storms. The snowfall rarely ceased. In the Badlands and out on the rolling prairie, snow lay up to four feet in depth, and as the lower layers compacted, the powdery flakes on top went billowing with the constant wind like a thick whitish fog. Upon reaching the Badlands, the snow flowed down into ravines and coulees to form massive drifts, a hundred feet or more, which rose to prairie level, and it was as if the Badlands had disappeared. Those ranches located amongst the creeks and along the Little Missouri were covered over so that only chimneys marked the buildings, and countless numbers of cattle were buried alive.

January was just closing out its time upon the Badlands when still another blizzard struck down from the arctic, and for three days the wind screamed its fury. Anybody foolhardy enough to venture outside froze to death within minutes, while the cattle lucky enough to escape out of the Badlands and onto the prairie were simply blown over and died.

It wasn't until the third month of the year that out

of the west stole a chinook. Burning away the whitish haze was dazzling sunshine, shocking to the eyes of those now able to leave ranch buildings or towns. Out at the Hashknife, those who'd weathered out this winter were grateful to get outside. Still higher climbed the temperature, causing a great upheaval of snowmelt, and soon rivulets turned to a steady stream of water forming washouts and pouring out of gullies to seek creeks leading down to the Little Missouri River.

In a little while, Johnny Crowheart realized with a few misgivings, he would be leaving the Hashknife, and going with him would be Carrie Morgan. Their first stop would be down at that Baptist Church in Medora and a simple wedding ceremony. After that, with the thousand dollars Jake Murdock had pressed upon them, the west beckoned. Frankly, he hated to leave.

"Carrie, that you're alive still seems like a miracle to me."

"We've gone through a lot, my love. I can tell you want to stay around here. But, Johnny, for me there's too many painful memories. Can you understand that?"

"There are some for me, too. In another two weeks it'll be fit for traveling."

When they left, around the middle of March, it was to find themselves on a high bank above the Little Missouri, and to see a sight which would haunt them for a long time, for a flood-wave of debris was coming down the river flood plain causing a great roar. Mingled with the jagged chunks of river ice, that at first seemed to be nothing but more debris, came the carcasses of cattle that had perished during the winter, rolling over and over or being carried atop an ice floe, a river of death that brought over a few days thousands of dead cattle. When the ranchers and cowboys went out to see if any livestock had survived, they numbered only a handful. Later came the bone pickers with their wagons, to pick at the bones of what had once been great range herds.

At last, after keeping some distance away from the river, Crowheart and the woman he was to marry came loping toward Medora, and at a quiet word from him they drew up and brought their horses around. He let his eyes take in the quiet majesty of these sunken mountains, the Badlands, just beginning to cast off the yoke of winter, the winter of the blue snow. He knew that someday he'd be back.

"The hardy ones will survive," he said softly. "Men like Murdock and Bill Lowman. You mentioned something about Oregon?"

"That was a dream my pa had."

"Should we make it ours?"

"Just so we're together."

Touching spurs to their horses, they rode on into Medora and a new beginning.

POWELL'S ARMY
BY TERENCE DUNCAN

#1: UNCHAINED LIGHTNING (1994, $2.50)

Thundering out of the past, a trio of deadly enforcers dispenses its own brand of frontier justice throughout the untamed American West! Two men and one woman, they are the U.S. Army's most lethal secret weapon—they are POWELL'S ARMY!

#2: APACHE RAIDERS (2073, $2.50)

The disappearance of seventeen Apache maidens brings tribal unrest to the violent breaking point. To prevent an explosion of bloodshed, Powell's Army races through a nightmare world south of the border—and into the deadly clutches of a vicious band of Mexican flesh merchants!

#3: MUSTANG WARRIORS (2171, $2.50)

Someone is selling cavalry guns and horses to the Comanche—and that spells trouble for the bluecoats' campaign against Chief Quanah Parker's bloodthirsty Kwahadi warriors. But Powell's Army are no strangers to trouble. When the showdown comes, they'll be ready—and someone is going to die!

#4: ROBBERS ROOST (2285, $2.50)

After hijacking an army payroll wagon and killing the troopers riding guard, Three-Fingered Jack and his gang high-tail it into Virginia City to spend their ill-gotten gains. But Powell's Army plans to apprehend the murderous hardcases before the local vigilantes do—to make sure that Jack and his slimy band stretch hemp the legal way!

Available wherever paperbacks are sold, or order direct from the Publisher. Send cover price plus 50¢ per copy for mailing and handling to Zebra Books, Dept. 2432, 475 Park Avenue South, New York, N.Y. 10016. Residents of New York, New Jersey and Pennsylvania must include sales tax. DO NOT SEND CASH.

BOLD HEROES OF THE UNTAMED NORTHWEST!
THE SCARLET RIDERS
by Ian Anderson

#1: CORPORAL CAVANNAGH (1161, $2.50)
Joining the Mounties was Cavannagh's last chance at a new life. Now he would stop either an Indian war, or a bullet—and out of his daring and courage a legend would be born!

#3: BEYOND THE STONE HEAPS (1884, $2.50)
Fresh from the slaughter at the Little Big Horn, the Sioux cross the border into Canada. Only Cavannagh can prevent the raging Indian war that threatens to destroy the Scarlet Riders!

#4: SERGEANT O'REILLY (1977, $2.50)
When an Indian village is reduced to ashes, Sergeant O'Reilly of the Mounties risks his life and career to help an avenging Stoney chief and bring a silver-hungry murderer to justice!

#5: FORT TERROR (2125, $2.50)
Captured by the robed and bearded killer monks of Fort Terror, Parsons knew it was up to him, and him alone, to stop a terrifying reign of anarchy and chaos by the deadliest assassins in the territory—and continue the growing legend of The Scarlet Riders!

Available wherever paperbacks are sold, or order direct from the Publisher. Send cover price plus 50¢ per copy for mailing and handling to Zebra Books, Dept. 2432, 475 Park Avenue South, New York, N.Y. 10016. Residents of New York, New Jersey and Pennsylvania must include sales tax. DO NOT SEND CASH.